NEPTIA'S GALAXY RAILWAY

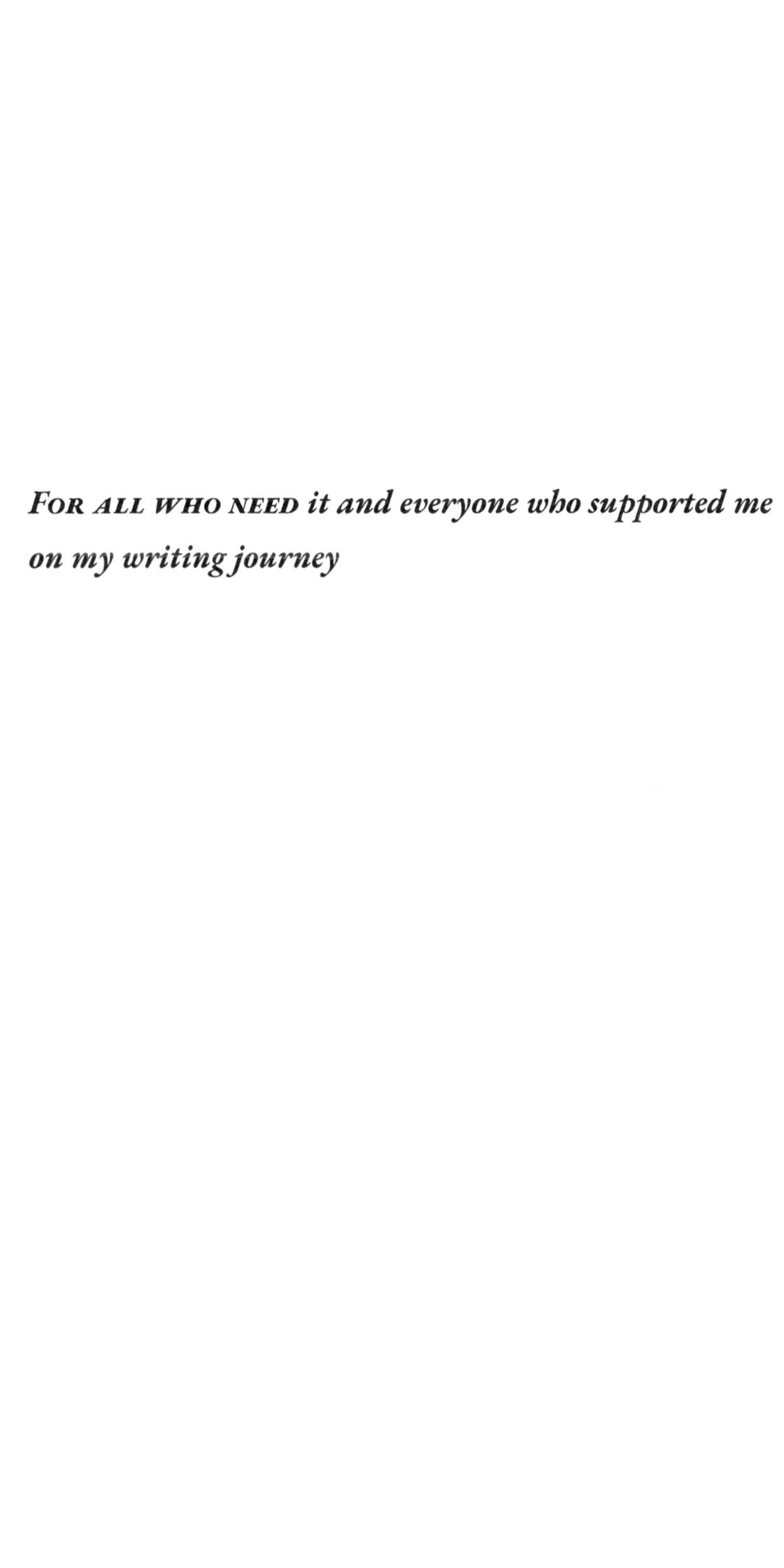

FOR ALL WHO NEED it and everyone who supported me on my writing journey

CHAPTER ONE

"Stop right there!"

A stowaway dashes through a crowded train station, running and hopping over trains. Station guards, having been notified of this stowaway and his ability to elude the authorities, give chase. Our stowaway ducks and dodges away from the station police - pushing people over and throwing trash cans on their side - all while his pursuers yell at him to stop. He eventually finds a large group of well-dressed travelers and sinks into them, invisible in the crowd. Finally, after what seems like an eternity, the police pass him by.

Our story's setting does not involve a railway from a day in our time. This is a railway that travels through space with the ease of trains from the current year, yet reaches the destination in even less time.

So, how did we get here?

Long before the events of this story, humanity became space-faring, terraforming Earth's moon, Mars, and Venus into liveable planets like Earth (or Terra for the new-age folk). Once humanity was able to send a man-led mission to the closest planet outside of their solar system - Proxima Centauri b - and successfully terraformed it, they began to expand to other parts of the galaxy, discovering new planets, resources, and fantastic species that most would never dream of. While many of these meetings of the more sentient species were met with hostility, a vast majority were successful, leading to a golden age for humanity, and the species who accepted them with open arms. However, not all was exactly perfect for humanity as it branched to the edges of the galaxy.

After a series of failed explorations that resulted in casualties, humanity and other allied species of the galaxy decided that there needed to be a safer way to research, discover, and terraform planets while also improving travel conditions to ones that had already been discovered, and thus, the IRTD (Intergalactic Research and Travel Department) was born, offering information to travelers about a planet's history, how it was structured, and even some helpful tips for those who might be staying on a planet for long periods of time. The IRTD comprised the best researchers and adventurers of the galaxy, and four years after its creation, the first commercial travel ships for multiple travelers were created and made available for public use. These ships would make stops at stations on various planets that the IRTD deemed safe for travel. With a simple ticket for boarding, this reduced the need for personal ships. Some years later, an engineer from the IRTD, Darrius Timalra, became bored of the typical rectangular gray metal ships lined with seating and decided to offer something that had been commonplace where his descendants came from:

Trains from Earth.

After some years of work, the first commercial galactic train flew into the Ridgehall University for Spaceship Studies and Engineering on Viona, where it would successfully take off from the planet and begin a new age of space travel and comfort. Timalra's train was a massive success, resulting in the creation of three more galactic trains for commercial travel across the galaxy.

As the IRTD was planning to build a fourth galactic train, a man by the name of Linus Goldstar of the Goldstar Mining Company threw his hat into the ring and offered to make the galactic train. After some discussions, and regulations checks, the first galactic train made by a company other than the IRTD - the luxurious Goldstar line of trains - was created. After the Goldstar train was made available, more companies followed suit, causing the metal travel ships from the IRTD to become obsolete. Company trains, along with the three that the IRTD created, became the norm for intergalactic travel, creating a system where companies held a monopoly on travel to certain planets.

Some of these trains consist of Greencoal, Hyphen-Tak, and Myiliga: low-class train lines just used to get from point A to point b. Rivetclick, Lunafeild, and Alpha-Century lines are far better than the low-class trains and are often viewed as trains for longer distances. And finally, Asturon, Moonriver, and the Goldstar lines are the highest class of trains one can even dream of riding, with the Goldstar line being rated as the best of the best for travelers.

The stowaway looks around and lets out a sigh of relief, knowing the guards have given up the chase for a while. The group around him begins to move, and he quickly runs toward the slightly ajar doors leading to a train platform, almost tripping as he barges in. Once he recovers, he finds himself on a platform of black marble with edges of pure gold.

The stowaway looks up to find the platform separated from the vacuum of space outside by a wall of glass across the tracks where a row of planets crookedly circles a sun. He isn't able to marvel at the beauty of the circling planets for very long, as a whistle from the distance pulls him back to reality. He glances to the left to see a black and gold train pulling into the station, the title, GOLDSTAR etched on the side in gold. The train opens its doors as our stowaway contemplates climbing aboard.

He doesn't know what the train holds; it could just be another view of the galaxy around him–

"I saw him go through here!!" a voice yells from behind him "C'mon! Let's go!!"

Station guards again.

The stowaway quickly forges into the crowd and onboard the train, rushing toward the back compartments. He makes it to the second-to-last trolley and hides under a table, covering himself with his grayish-black, wool trench coat. This outfit makes him almost identical to the other riders of the galaxy's railway, allowing for an easy disguise from authorities.

As our hideaway peeks out from under his table, he observes that the interior of the train is an elegant blend of gold and black. The seats and tables follow the theme: smooth black and edged with gold. The only places where this peculiar theme isn't followed are the walls of the train, where a lighter shade of yellow adorned with dandelion-like designs makes its appearance.

A whistle from the outside is heard and the train starts to chug forward, leaving the station. As the vehicle begins to build up to maximum speed, it travels through space as if it were a normal train on a track. The stowaway stands from his crouching position under the table, carefully setting the gray backpack that's been hugging his back on the seat next to him.

He looks out the window to see the train is leaving the solar system at a decent pace.

As he surveys his surroundings, his reflection stares back at him, and the stowaway gets a good look at himself for the first time in a while. His skin is slightly sun-kissed, and his eyes are brown. He combs through his jet-black hair for anything out of the ordinary. After that is done, he pushes the medium-length hair behind his left ear and studies a tag that is hanging on the lobe of it. It has a symbol that he's never seen before, etched in green on a brown plastic that wouldn't be out of place on a cow at a dairy farm, or whatever alien creature is used for milk in this day and age.

"Hi!"

He jumps and turns his attention to a girl looking at him over the seat in front of him. Her skin is slightly dark and her eyes are bright green in color. Her hair is similar in texture to an afro and pulled back into a bun with a bright blue scrunchie.

He takes a deep breath and lets out a nervous, "Hi."

"The name's Neptia Goldstar!" she says brightly, holding out a hand.

He takes her hand, and squinting slightly, tilts his head.

"Are...are you related to the people that own this train line?"

"Mhm!" She nods, still wearing a smile. "What's your name?"

He opens his mouth to say something but quickly closes it. A confused look crosses his face.

"I...don't think I have a name," he says.

Neptia jumps back a bit and opens her eyes wide in surprise.

"Everyone has a name! How do you not have one?"

He just shrugs, a smirk on his face, as he throws his hands up in an "I dunno" gesture.

"Well, I'm going to give you a name. Here and now."

"You don't have to. Really," he protests.

"No, it's alright. I don't mind. How about...Montag?"

He tilts his head in confusion.

"Montag?" he asks.

"Yeah! Montag! It's from this book - *Fahrenheit 451*..."

She rummages through her bag and pulls out a copy of the book, holding it out in front of him.

"I stole it from someone's luggage!"

He frowns disapprovingly. "You shouldn't steal."

"Do you like Montag as a name, though?"

"No."

"Monty?"

"No."

"Mortimer?"

"Let's leave the "M" names alone."

After rattling off names and having each and every one rejected, Neptia finally says, "Tavvi".

He opens his eyes a bit, considers, and nods. "That sounds nice."

Nep smiles and giggles a bit. "I got it from the tag in your ear."

"It's nice. I want that name," Tavvi decides.

"Great! Your name is now Tavvi!"

Tavvi nods at her once more before Nep sinks back into her seat and starts to rummage around in her bag, pulling out something resembling a compact and fiddling with it. Tavvi looks back at the window, the train flying past stars so fast they almost look like snowflakes in a nighttime snowstorm. He closes his eyes and sighs.

"So," he asks Neptia. "Where are you headed?"

Neptia jumps back in her seat and peeks over at Tavvi. "I'm going to the last stop and taking the Goldstar Line from there,"

Tavvi makes a sound of approval and nods.

"You wanna tag along?" she asks.

Tavvi opens his eyes wide and thinks for a moment. He wouldn't be stuck running around stations, chased after by station guards. Plus, he wouldn't be alone in the vastness of space. There were more pros than cons in this situation.

"Sure!" he agrees. "But on one condition."

"What's that?"

"You buy my tickets."

"Oh..."

Nep takes a sharp breath in and looks away.

"I don't know if I can do that..." she trails off.

"Why not?" Tavvi asks, concerned.

"Because..." Neptia says through clenched teeth. "I'm a stowaway and I can barely afford to live on the planets at the end of the line..."

"WAIT, what?!" Tavvi yells out, shocked.

"Oh, it's not that bad. I've been doing this for years."

"Years?!" Tavvi yells. "How many?!"

"About three. Why does that bother you so much, anyways?"

"I'm a stowaway too!"

Neptia's eyes glow with excitement, and she taps her hands on the back of the seat as she smiles.

"No way!" she screeches. "What planet are you from?"

Tavvi calms down after a moment and rubs his face.

"I...I don't really remember," he admits. "The only thing I remember is waking up on the Greencoal Line with this freaking tag in my ear and a black eye. That's all I really know."

Nep opens her mouth to ask something else, but four loud bings play over the intercom of the train. The pair turn their attention to one of the speakers located on the ceiling of the trolly car.

"*Good day, riders. This is your conductor,*"a voice blares out. "*We are currently at our last stop: Lethum. We ask that you please exit the train once we come to a complete stop, and we thank you again for choosing the GoldStar Line for your choice of travel.*"

No sooner is the message completed, then Neptia begins getting ready to exit the train.

"Wait," Tavvi says. "What are you going to do on Lethum?"

"I'm going to get a cheap hotel room..." she says. "And I'm gonna stay there until the next Goldstar Train comes to the planet."

She gets her belongings together and stands, looking at Tavvi.

"Have you decided if you wanna tag along?" she asks him again. "I can't get us tickets, but I can get us a room and some food. That's just as good, right?"

Tavvi puts his head down and sighs. He knows it would be better to stick with her instead of running around a station aimlessly with the possibility of station guards coming after him every time he leaves the train.

"Fine," Tavvi says, raising his head. "I'll come along."

He stands up and slips his backpack onto his back. The train comes to a complete stop and the doors open with a familiar echo of, "*Please stand behind the yellow lines.*". Before they leave the station, Neptia drags Tavvi over to a wall of lockers behind the information desk.

"Do you have something in one of these?" Tavvi asks.

"Not yet," she says, rummaging through a couple of lockers.

She opens a third locker and finds a hotel key. Smiling brightly, she jingles it in front of Tavvi.

"Free hotel for us!" she exclaims. "Let's get outta here!"

CHAPTER TWO

REPORT ON LETHUM....INCOMING...READY...

Lethum is the third planet in the Brye Solar System. It has a deep purple hue from the gasses found on the planet. However, due to these gasses, Lethum is not a safe destination for most of the beings living in the galaxy. Thankfully, after many years of research and development, glass biodomes filled with safe, breathable air have been implemented on the planet! Travel to each of the 10 (and growing!) biodomes can be accessed via monorails which connect the biodomes like a molecular compound model.

For more information about tickets and accessing the monorail, please contact...

After leaving the station, Neptia begins her search for the hotel, innocently explaining to the locals: "I was supposed to meet my friend at this hotel, but they didn't tell me where it's located. Do you know where it's at?"

Meanwhile, Tavvi stays close, silently observing the planet and its inhabitants.

Tavvi wonders if the people living here are living in a state of fear, constantly aware that one crack in any of the biodomes could possibly end their lives, their livelihoods, and their families. He is snapped out of these thoughts as Neptia bounds over to inform him they'll have to take the monorail to the hotel.

"Also," she adds, meandering through the crowds to the nearest monorail station, "this isn't the prettiest planet in the galaxy."

Tavvi tilts his head in confusion, curious as to why.

Neptia simply states: "It's not supposed to be."

Tavvi is now even more bewildered, but the instant he opens his mouth, Neptia cuts him off, telling him they need to hurry to the monorail before it leaves.

They make it to one of the stations and locate the monorail that will take them to the biodome where their hotel is located. The pair then sneak through the station, hop over the ticket gate, and narrowly avoid being crushed in the monorail's doors as it prepares for departure.

As the monorail travels the planet, Neptia and Tavvi study the area surrounding them. It is an odd sight between the deadly purple-colored gasses and the glass of the biodomes in the distance, each habitat creating the illusion of miniature blue skies for the people inside. They stand in silent awe for a bit before Tavvi sighs.

"Hey, Neptia?" Tavvi asks. "What did you mean about the planet being pretty earlier? When you said it's not supposed to be?"

"Oh, that," she says, shrugging her shoulders. "Planets that aren't supposed to be discovered and colonized aren't that pretty. I mean, look at this planet before we found it. Desolate, full of unbreathable air."

She looks out the window, staring at the surface of the planet. "We're not supposed to be standing on this planet."

Tavvi blinks, mystified and confused. He rubs his mouth before asking if he'll get fed more of that philosophy every time they land on a planet. Neptia lets out a laugh, assuring him he won't.

Soon, the monorail arrives at the hotel's biodome, and the stowaways exit with the crowd as it scurries to leave the monorail station. Neptia takes the lead and helps guide them to the hotel in the middle of a city.

The hotel is a simple red and gold building on the outside, making it easy to track down amid the white three-story buildings that populate this particular biodome. They enter the hotel and are greeted by a red interior with a plush oriental rug beneath them and a warm "Welcome!" from the doorman. Neptia saunters up to the concierge desk and asks where the room is located as Tavvi looks around the lobby.

Usually, Tavvi would end up sleeping somewhere in the stations, covering his face so the station police could not recognize him. He has to admit this is a nice change of pace. Deep in thought, he pushes back some of the hair that has fallen out of place, and as his finger hits the tag in his ear, he hears someone whisper next to him. Jumping in alarm, Tavvi whips around to find no one beside him.

Once more, he touches the tag in his ear and hears the whisper again. Growing more and more confused, he thumps down on the couch across from the concierge desk and holds his pointer finger, middle finger, and thumb on the tag, attempting to listen to the growing murmurs and whispers. Tavvi can't make out every word being said but what he can hear sounds like something about a "ritual," "going to another planet," and "becoming something greater than the universe itself".

He soon hears the snapping of someone's fingers in front of him and comes out of his trance to find Neptia staring down at him.

"I found where our room is," she says. "Let's go."

Tavvi nods and follows his new friend to the room, holding his head. Neptia looks back at him as they walk, concerned.

"You okay?" she questions worriedly. "Were you thinking about something in the lobby?"

Tavvi looks at Neptia and rubs his head.

"Nah," he replies. "I'm just tired."

It's a lie, but Neptia takes it, and they continue the walk to their room. Finally reaching it, Neptia opens the door to reveal a simple room with a single bed, sofa, and recliner. Tavvi walks into the room first and shakes off his backpack before falling down on the recliner. Neptia studies her new friend from her perch on the bed.

"Do you have a headache?" she asks, troubled. "I have some medicine for that."

Tavvi only shakes his head, resting it on his hand and nodding off. Neptia hops off the bed and ambles over to tap his forehead. He snaps awake again, his eyes wide.

"What's wrong?" he asks.

"Nothing!" she replies, putting her hands up. "Just wanted to say the next Goldstar Train will be here in two days, early in the morning, okay?"

CHAPTER THREE

TAVVI WAKES UP IN a cave engulfed in black. As he blinks and rubs his eyes open, he concludes that he must be dreaming. He raises his head to find the dark cave overlooking a cliff. Slowly, he rises and walks out onto the cliff.

The only light source is a pure, white moon in the sky, outlining everything it touches in silver. Tavvi cautiously walks to the edge of the cliff and peers out into the distance, attempting to see anything beyond. He quickly notices the moonlight growing in intensity around him, ridding the area of its silver outline. He looks up to find the moon leaving the sky and approaching him.

He reaches out to touch it, but before he can, the moon explodes in a brilliant flash of white, and ribbon-like streaks materialize from within it. Tavvi covers his face protectively with his right arm and backs away. As the explosion dissipates, he discovers the moon has become a glowing, white silhouette of a woman adorned in something akin to a long ballroom dress with a flowing jacket, her loose hair flowing where the moon had exploded seconds before. She has no discernible facial features: no nose, eyes, or mouth.

Tavvi approaches the silhouette, mystified. As he walks closer, the woman reaches out and cups Tavvi's face in her hands. Tavvi feels himself relax, slowly closing his eyes. She rubs his cheeks with her thumbs for a few moments before the cliff explodes in another brilliant flash of white, waking Tavvi up with a shock.

On the recliner, Tavvi lets out a yelp upon waking, rousing Neptia with the same energy. She sits up in bed, eyes wide, while Tavvi groans and rubs his face.

"Nightmare?" Neptia asks.

"I-I don't know," Tavvi stammers.

Nep blinks for a bit before lifting her pillow and grabbing her computer compact to check the time.

"Two twenty-six," she announces groggily. "Breakfast won't be served until seven. Try to go back to sleep, okay?"

Tavvi makes a soft sound of approval before sliding out of the chair and walking to the sofa to lie down, falling back asleep instantly.

"Tavvi?"

Tavvi wakes to find Neptia standing over him with a small smile.

"It's seven. Breakfast is served!" she cheers. "Let's go grab a bite, and then we can go look around the planet!" Tavvi groans and pushes himself up, passing Neptia and heading straight for the shower.

"Do you want me to wait for you?" she asks.

He pokes his head out of the bathroom and shrugs.

"Not in the mood to talk this morning?"

"Let me take a shower, and I'll get back to you," he replies.

"Gotcha!"

Tavvi closes the door and turns the shower on, running his fingers under the water to check the temperature. After it's to his liking, he undresses and climbs under the water spray. As the water runs over him, he touches the tag in his ear again, hearing the same persistent murmurs from yesterday. He decides it isn't worth the trouble to keep listening at the moment, so he washes quickly and climbs out.

After he finishes drying and dressing, he leaves the bathroom to find Neptia perched on the bed looking at her compact computer. She glances up and asks Tavvi if he's ready to go, and they leave the hotel room. They migrate to the hotel dining room to find a buffet of food around the room. Neptia points out the food for humans, and they serve themselves and sit down at a table.

Not much is said over the meal, other than Neptia questioning if Tavvi has ever been here, to which he says he doesn't remember. Once they finish eating, the duo leaves the hotel and begins to explore the planet. Their first stop is a small museum filled with artifacts from Lethum prior to its colonization. This is followed by a visit to a small shop filled with souvenirs and other knick-knacks.

"Is this all you do when you visit planets, Nep?" Tavvi asks, inspecting a music box.

"Pretty much," Neptia confirms. "I try to keep a low profile, and this is how I do it."

Tavvi makes a sound of approval before continuing to look around. As they finish their perusal of the shop, he asks what's next on their agenda. Neptia has her heart set on exploring another nearby museum, and Tavvi shrugs in agreement, following her out the door. This continues for several more stops.

After yet another museum visit, they relax on a bench overlooking a river. Neptia hums to herself, tapping on her compact computer, while Tavvi looks across the river to another city. He touches the tag in his ear again and listens to the murmurs in his head, still trying to decode what they're saying.

Neptia puts her compact computer away and looks to her right. She suddenly gasps and shakes Tavvi's shoulder, rudely knocking him out of his trance.

"Tavvi look!" she squeals with a smile.

She points to a sign, and Tavvi follows her finger to an advertisement outside a shop that reads: "Free fortunes for intergalactic visitors! Limited time only!"

Tavvi studies the poster skeptically. "I dunno about this, Nep," he begins. "It could be a scam—"

"C'mon don't be a square!" She grabs his arm despite his protests and practically drags him inside the fortune teller's store.

Neptia pulls back the curtains disguising the entrance to reveal a shop cluttered with various herbs and antiques.

"Welcome! Welcome!" a voice crow from the back of the building.

A small elderly woman wearing a patchwork dress appears from behind another set of curtains located in the back of the shop, apparently there to separate the store from her living quarters. Neptia smiles and approaches the woman.

"And how can I help you two today?" the shopkeeper asks.

"We're here for the free fortune-telling," Neptia announces happily.

"Ah, yes, yes!" the woman agrees. "Come to this table."

They walk to a table situated in the middle of the room and covered in a purple cloth patterned with constellations. Tavvi stands nearby doubtfully as Neptia takes a seat in the chair in front of the table opposite the old woman. She asks for Neptia's palm and Nep acquiesces with a grin. The woman runs her middle and index finger across the palm of Neptia's right hand, smiling with her eyes closed.

"I see you come from a wealthy family!" she says cheerfully.

"I do!" Neptia confirms.

The woman continues to probe Neptia's palm, making a low humming sound as she thinks.

"From what I see, you will be a very beloved and beautiful woman if you continue on the path you're going!"

Neptia looks back at Tavvi and smirks. Tavvi rolls his eyes in response and crosses his arms.

"And from what the stars say, you should try to keep a small piece of that wealth to yourself, do not share it with anyone,"

"Why?" Neptia questions.

"It will be needed in the future. I'm not sure why, though. The stars are not cooperating today."

She opens her eyes and looks at Neptia. "You have a lot of good in you. Don't let anyone take you for granted, okay?"

Neptia smiles and nods while the woman inspects Tavvi.

"Would your friend here like–?"

Her eyes widen as she sees the tag in Tavvi's ear. In a panic, the fortuneteller stands up and dashes over to him. With a trembling hand, she wraps Tavvi's tag in her hand as he flinches and looks at her agitatedly.

"What the hell are you doing?!" Tavvi demands.

She doesn't say anything, but as she finally releases his tag, she covers her mouth and points at him.

"Y-you're…" she stammers out. "You're from the Nylat Solar System."

Neptia gets up from her seat and walks over to the woman. "Do you know what planet in that system he's from?"

Still trembling, the old woman places her left hand on Tavvi's tag and her right on her forehead.

"Rialea."

Neptia turns to Tavvi and gives him a nod and confident smile, which Tavvi returns.

"Do you know anything else about me?" Tavvi asks. "I lost my memories and have no idea who I am."

"You'll regain your memories if you manage to travel to that solar system. Remember. Nylat Solar System. Rialca. Good luck."

"Do you know anything else?"

She shakes her head and sighs. "I can only tell you where to go for answers."

Tavvi looks to the side and groans in disappointment. He huffs again and turns his attention to Neptia, who is murmuring something to the fortune teller. He comes to the conclusion that a random stranger can't possibly have the answer for who he is. He'll have to find that answer on his own. It might take some time, but he'll find it. Hopefully.

"Let's go, Tavvi," Neptia urges, tapping him on his left arm and walking toward the exit.

Tavvi follows her outside. They walk for a little way before Neptia smiles and shakes her hands in excitement.

"I can't wait to see what your planet looks like!" she exclaims.

Tavvi makes a sound of agreement. "And I can't wait to see what my real name is," he replies. "What's next?"

Neptia digs into her pocket and pulls out some slips of paper resembling train tickets.

"Money time," She says cryptically. "I'm going to resell these and get us some quick cash."

"Isn't that illegal?"

"Not until someone calls the cops."

CHAPTER FOUR

Lethum's morning sun has just risen when the alarm on Neptia's computer compact wakes her up. She sits up and stretches before walking over to Tavvi on the couch to shake him awake. When the two finally leave the hotel room, they climb aboard the monorail that travels to the railway station. Upon their arrival at the station, the duo ventures inside, but before they can walk to the Goldstar Platform, Neptia holds up her hand and gestures for Tavvi to wait.

She brightens at her new idea. "We can skip the train and use the Planet Teleporter to get to Rialea instead!"

The Universal Planet Teleporter (or UPT) is a device found in railway stations that allows travel to other planets without the use of a train. All that's needed are the destination's coordinates and a small one-time fee. Then, you enter the elevator, and boom! You're at your destination!

Neptia and Tavvi walk over to the information desk where they are greeted by a navigator with a warm smile on her face.

"Hello!" the navigator chirps. "How can I help you to-day?"

"Hi!" Neptia replies. "We're looking for a planet…"

"Great! Do you have a name?"

"Rialea."

The navigator types something on the computer behind the desk and gives a small frown before turning her attention back to the duo.

"I can't seem to find that planet," she says. "Do you have any information on it?"

"It's in the Nylat Solar System," Tavvi replies anxiously.

The navigator thanks him and goes back to typing. However, she soon shakes her head and looks at the duo apologetically.

"I'm still not finding anything," she says. "Do you know any planets or solar systems close to it? That way we can see if there's anything we can work with and get a route ready for you."

"No," Neptia says, a little saddened. "Thank you."

Nep leaves the counter with Tavvi behind her. She sighs and starts to walk toward the Goldstar Platform.

"What are you going to do now?" Tavvi asks, tailing behind her.

"Let's just keep traveling the Goldstar Line!" she exclaims, brightening up and turning around to him. "Maybe we'll find a planet or something that's nearby. That's the glory of space! It's vast and infinite! We haven't even scratched the surface of how far we can travel! Your home is out there somewhere, we just have to look! It may take us some time, but we'll find it! Because with the power of the grand Goldstar Line, we'll get..."

Tavvi, by this point, has stopped listening. He walks past his friend to the Goldstar Platform, climbing aboard a waiting train. Neptia stops her speech, screeching that she wasn't done as she follows him to the next planet.

"HMMM, LET ME ROLL back the video from a few minutes ago," the navigator mumbles, typing away on her computer.

Behind her, two station officers peer down at the screen. They were notified by an anonymous tip that Neptia and Tavvi had been spotted at this station boarding a train for another planet.

The first officer - Rayard - is a typical humanoid with somewhat pale skin, black eyes, and dark brown hair that appears black in certain lights. His partner Verla, on the other hand, gives a much different impression. She is a type of species known as Osanus. These beings have a humanoid shape and features, but the comparison ends there with their indigo skin, white hair, and pointy ears.

Verla is no exception. Despite the similarities to others of her species, however, Verla's eyes are striking. Her pupils are white, with the remainder of her eye appearing as black as space.

"Wait!" Verla exclaims, pointing a finger at the screen. "Stop it, right there!"

The navigator pauses the video and it freezes on footage of Neptia following Tavvi across the Goldstar Platform.

"That's her, right?" Verla asks.

Ray nods.

"Roll the footage back a few seconds" Ray orders.

The navigator nods and rolls it back, pausing as Tavvi walks onto the platform. Rayard sighs and crosses his arms.

"That's the stowaway from the Namoah station, right?" Verla asks.

Ray offers a nod and makes a sound of approval.

"They're probably working together..." he speculates.

"Looks like they got on the Goldstar Line to Viona," the navigator says.

"Viona, huh?" Verla ponders. "That's a good two-to-three-hour ride."

Ray nods once again. "Thank you for your help," he says, addressing the navigator. "If you see them again, call us."

The navigator nods her head in confirmation as the two officers walk away from the desk.

Verla sighs and stretches. "So, now what?" she asks.

"Wait for HQ and go from there," Ray answers. "Can't chase someone without clearance."

A melody begins to play from the computer compact Ray keeps on his shoulder. "There we go."

He twists the compact and it detaches into his hand, a holographic image of another officer appearing in front of them.

"Ray and Verla here," Ray says, saluting.

"This is Headquarters," the officer responds. "You two have been granted permission to go after the individuals known as "Neptia Goldstar" and "The Unknown Stowaway." But proceed with caution! They could be armed."

"Thank you," Ray says. "Ray and Verla out!"

He salutes, and the hologram vanishes. Ray struts through the crowds with a small smile.

"That reminds me," Verla says. "I went to Viona for a vacation one time. It was nice."

"Yeah," Ray concurs. "And what else'll be nice is the windfall we get from Little Miss Goldstar."

Verla sighs and rolls her eyes. This was going to be a long case.

CHAPTER FIVE

Report on Viona...incoming...ready...

Viona is the seventh planet in the Prouscul Solar System. This world is comprised of many layers floating above each other. Each layer is a different color, making it easy to travel and locate various facilities and landmarks. There are currently ten known layers to Viona, beginning with White. Traveling to each layer is as simple as falling to the level you wish to visit via the free Viovators located on the planet.

For more information about hot locations or the "Ten-minute, Ten-layer Challenge" please visit...

As Tavvi and Neptia leave the station, Neptia raises her arms to gesture around them.

"Now this is a planet!" she exclaims. She quickly begins her usual shenanigans of scalping people for tickets, as Tavvi lurks nearby.

After swindling a few poor tourists out of some money, the duo stops at a restaurant to grab a bite to eat. They find a seat, and Neptia inspects Tavvi as she rests her head on her hands. Two menus are plopped on the table, and Tavvi grabs one in an attempt to avoid the questioning eyes across from him.

"Do you have any of your memories back?" Neptia finally asks.

Tavvi shakes his head, engrossed in the menu. After a few more minutes of being watched, he sighs.

"Are you really related to the Goldstar Line?" he asks. "Or do you just say that for fun?"

She simply nods with an accompanying, "Uh-huh."

"Uh-huh to which question?"

"I'm a Goldstar."

"Why did you run away, then?"

Neptia's smile fades, and she looks out the window, dropping her arms in front of her.

"I just got tired of my family," she says quietly. "They were always trying to reach 'the center of the universe' with the train. I hated it."

"What do you mean by that?"

"Well…my family is trying to connect the Goldstar Line to every planet in the universe."

"That doesn't sound so bad," Tavvi remarks. "That way more people can travel."

"Yes, it is," she disagrees, interrupting. "Remember what I said on Lethum? Not all planets are supposed to be discovered! They shouldn't be discovered."

Tavvi begins to open his mouth to ask a question, but Neptia has already called the waiter over to order, her menu blocking her face from Tavvi's view. They eat their meal in silence, curry, a grilled three-cheese sandwich, and creamy tomato soup sitting awkwardly between them.

After the meal, Neptia and Tavvi conduct a brief, but unsuccessful search as to the known whereabouts of Rialea. Along the way, they find a hotel to frequent for the next few days, but as they enter the lobby, something on the entrance's bulletin board catches Neptia's eye. She walks over and points out a wanted poster with their faces that reads: "WANTED! STOWAWAYS! Wanted by the Intergalactic Safety and Protection Department (ISPD)! If you have any information about these two, please contact the authorities immediately!"

Neptia chuckles and rips the poster up, tossing the shreds into a trashcan next to the board.

"No one ever reports stowaways," she says, still scoffing. "I mean, look at me, still running free!"

The person working the front desk appears from a backroom and asks if he can offer the newcomers any assistance. They ask for a room, then head down a hallway to their quarters to get settled. Once in the room, Neptia pulls out her computer compact and studies a map of the current star system.

"So," she begins. "How do we find information about a planet that not even the stations know about?"

"This sounds like a paradoxical question," Tavvi remarks. "Maybe we could just ask around like we planned, but that might take a while."

"That's what I was thinking, too," she says. "Space is infinite. We could be asking around until we're damn near eighty..."

"We could just ask for ballpark estimates. Maybe Rialea is a remote planet. Like it's only known by a few people here and there."

"And where are those people?"

Taavi starts to speak but closes his mouth. He raises a finger, thinking hard.

"I think we'll be traveling around for a while," Neptia says, closing the map. "I'm gonna have a shower and think about what to do next, or did you want to?"

Tavvi shakes his head, and Neptia walks into the bathroom. She calmly undresses and steps into the bathtub, letting the warm water run over her. She sighs to herself and looks up.

How the hell do we even know that planet exists? she thinks to herself. *I'm really having second thoughts about tagging along with this guy. I wonder if I should just leave...* She shakes her head and laughs. *Nah, it's good to have two people together when you're stowing away. Even if he has amnesia. Or maybe I'll just leave. No, don't be stupid, Nep.*

She turns off the shower and dries herself off, changing into her pajamas. *If he tries anything funny, or if he's too weird, then you bolt.*

She opens the shower door to find Tavvi sleeping on the bed. She walks over to him and puts a hand near his shoulder, but quickly pulls back, deciding it would be better to let him sleep. Neptia lets out a sigh and folds out the mattress from the sofa.

TAVVI WAKES SLOWLY TO find himself looking up at a roof made of white glass. He sits up in surprise to see the inside of a mansion with walls and doors of gold. The floor is an interesting mix of white with black speckles splashed on top, the tiles cut into hexagonal shapes. Tavvi is aware he is dreaming, but he is comforted to find that he is not overlooking a cliff like last time. He jolts to his feet at the sound of an argument from a nearby room.

Rushing over to one of the room's doors, he puts his ear to it, hearing a group of people arguing on the other side. Tavvi enters the room and finds it adorned with plush stuffed animals. A small bed sits on the left side of the room with a desk to the right. In front of him, three figures flicker like a memory. Although hard to make out, the shapes are of a woman and a man, both adults, frowning down at another shadow. One of another woman. Possibly a teenager?

The man has his back turned to the woman and appears to be wearing something like a suit. The woman, meanwhile, is wearing a sort of elegant dress. Is a ball or something about to start? The teenager appears less formal, dressed in something like a school uniform.

"Did I hear you correctly?" The dress-wearing figure shouts. "You got kicked out of the academy AGAIN?! What did you do this time?!"

The teenager speaks, but no words come out. Her mouth moves, but no noise can be heard.

"This is a new one. Why are you doing this? Is this NOT the school you want to go to?"

The teenager's mouth moves again.

"Well, what would you like to do?"

The smallest figure pauses for a moment, head tilted down, before speaking again. The figure of the man who has his back turned, crosses his arms tight and hangs his head in response.

"Out of the question. You will take over the family business! Put an end to that little thought you have!"

The teenage figure begins to say something else, but an index finger from the woman stops her, along with a fast "Up-up-up!" in an attempt to command silence. "No more!"

The teenager tries to look down, but the woman puts a hand underneath her chin, drawing her head up so she can look at the child.

"I know this is a very tough time for you, but you are a Goldstar! You need to keep your head up toward the sky and think of the future! For yourself and the universe!"

"Neptia?" Tavvi asks.

The man who has his back turned walks out of view. The door closes behind Tavvi, causing him to jump and look around cautiously, before snapping his attention back to the two remaining figures.

"Now, I'm going to go across the hall to see how the party's going. I want you to be ready by the time I come back, okay?"

The woman places a kiss on the teenager's head before exiting the room, leaving the girl alone. The teenager starts to shake as she bends down, pulling two briefcases and a backpack from under her bed and stuffing them with clothes. Her figure leaves with a loud slam of the door. Tavvi shakes himself out of his stupor and quickly follows.

The teenager runs through the halls to the front door of the mansion. Just as she is about to grab the handle, the figure freezes and turns to look back. But she just as quickly shakes her head and runs out of the mansion, slamming the door behind her. That slam must have been pretty powerful, because the mansion crumbles into a million little cubes, leaving Tavvi to float into darkness with the cubes of the mansion floating along beside him.

As Tavvi floats along, the shining, white silhouette of the woman from the cliff floats across from him She is no longer faceless, her now discernible features wearing a smile. A brilliant flash of white occurs, and Tavvi wakes up, although not with a shock like last time. He calmly sits up in bed and rubs his face.

Weird, he says to himself. *Still not as bad as the last one.*

He climbs out of bed and walks over to the window. The planet is a wonderful blend of neon lights and total darkness from within the layers. He looks back at Neptia sleeping, knowing the dream was about her.

Is that why you left, Nep? You didn't want to run the Gold-star Line?

He huffs and rubs his face before turning his attention back to his bed. He decides it isn't best to get hung up on a weird dream. Plus, he needs as much sleep as possible if they are going to continue their search in the morning. When he turns his attention to his bed, the covers fling themselves back, almost inviting him back to–

Wait, what?

Tavvi rubs his eyes and looks at the bed again. The covers definitely moved when he thought of climbing back in. He groans at the idea of his blankets moving by themselves.

I must really be tired.

Chapter Six

On the planet of Viona, Ray and Verla can be found on the trail of the two stowaways, as they wander around, ask locals for information, and check security cameras for incriminating footage. However, after hours of a fruitless search, they decide to head back to the railway station to see if Neptia and Tavvi have tried to leave the planet.

"Hey, Ray?" Verla asks. "Are you *sure* that girl is Neptia Goldstar? Like, an actual Goldstar?"

"Yes!" Ray replies. "How many times do I have to tell you this? She is!"

"Okay, and what about the guy that she's with?"

"Oh, he's just a random stowaway that's been evading police and hitching rides on trains for the past month. No idea why they're together."

Verla shrugs and glances around at the shops as they walk. "This just seems like a stowaway situation with a big reward ..."

"Look, I want that reward more than anything or anyone else, and I'll be damned if anyone gets it before me."

Verla frowns. "Money is the route to the fall of the universe."

Ray looks at Verla with a face full of confusion, but Verla only smiles innocently in response.

"Tavvi!"

Tavvi wakes up with a shock to find Neptia looking at him with a slightly panicked expression on her face.

"We overslept!" she exclaims. "The Goldstar Train's gonna be leaving in an hour and a half!"

Tavvi jumps out of bed, now fully awake, as they gather their belongings and rush out of their room to the lobby to check out. Thankfully, their hotel is not too terribly far, so they make it to the station with about fifteen minutes to spare. They sit down on the benches next to the inside door to catch their breaths before continuing.

"We're pretty fast runners, huh?" Neptia chuckles out.

Tavvi only nods before struggling to his feet, having caught his breath. Neptia copies him and leads Tavvi to the Goldstar Platform.

Once at the station, Verla receives a call on her computer compact. She jumps a bit and fumbles it before answering.

"V-Verla and Rayard reporting!" she stammers out, saluting the holographic image of an officer.

"Verla, this is Takra," the officer states. "The stowaways you two have been tasked with taking in have been seen at the eastern side of the station. It looks like they're trying to get on a train to another planet. Proceed with caution."

"Thanks, Takra!" Ray exclaims. "Over and out!"

Verla quickly closes her computer compact, and the two station police rush to the eastern side of the station.

NEPTIA AND TAVVI WANDER the crowds, eventually reaching an empty hallway on the eastern side of the station.

"We're not that far," Neptia says. "We just gotta make–"

TWEEEEEEEEET!!

The duo turns around to find two officers behind them, one wearing a crooked grin on his face, the other with a whistle in her mouth.

"Gotcha!" Ray shouts with glee.

"Tavvi...run," Neptia says quietly, grabbing onto his arm. "RUN!"

The stowaways make a dash for freedom, Ray immediately giving pursuit. Verla follows close behind. The four of them sprint through the station, cutting through crowds, knocking over a few trash cans, and tripping people up.

"Quick! In here!" Neptia whisper-yells.

Tavvi looks over to see Neptia point at a storage closet. The duo squeezes inside and slams the door just as Verla and Ray reach them. Ray goes up to the door first, putting a finger to his lips. He quietly opens the door, expecting to see the criminals tucked somewhere in the back of the closet. Instead, he's met with a metal bucket to the head, sending him sprawling to the ground.

Verla dodges a mop handle as the stowaways speed off in the opposite direction. She hesitates only a moment before chasing after them. Meanwhile, Ray stands up and swears, taking off yet again.

The fugitives and their pursuers run down another hallway similar to where they began. As she runs, Neptia shifts her backpack off her back to reach a bottle filled with some sort of clear liquid. She opens the bottle and begins to spray a jet of liquid behind her in a zigzag pattern. "She's slowing down!" Verla cheers. "They think water'll stop me? I'll handle this!"

Verla speeds up as Ray yells for her to stop, but it's too late. As soon as Verla's boot hits the liquid, she goes sliding forward, causing Neptia and Tavvi to run to the side to let her pass. Verla hits the wall at the end of the hallway, as Ray curses loudly. He huffs to himself and lunges, trying to clear the liquid. At this point, Tavvi, still on the run, glances behind him to find that Ray has sprouted wings and is hovering slightly over the liquid.

What?!

Tavvi does a double take and... yep. Ray has managed to clear the liquid with the help of wings that look like the last few leaves on a branch during the autumn. Just as Tavvi tries to process what he's seeing, he feels a hand on his shirt, and Neptia's dragging him to the right. He looks up and sees the Goldstar Platform. They shove through the doors to find a crowd of people.

The stowaways hide among the crowd, heaving out breaths of relief. A few seconds later, Ray breaks through the platform doors and looks out over the crowd. He's about to enter the masses but stops when he hears the whistle of the train in the distance. The officer backs up a little bit and bangs his hand on the platform doors.

"Just you wait Little Miss Goldstar!" he roars out into the crowd. "I'll find you and your friend! I promise that! So, keep counting your days!"

Verla stumbles up behind him, rubbing her head and groaning.

"Who are you yelling at?" she asks, sounding groggy.

Ray lets out a sigh of defeat and looks at his partner.

"No one," he says, frustrated. "Do you know where this train's stops are?"

"Yeah, I think so."

The station officers leave the platform as the train pulls in, hoping to regroup and resume their chase slightly later.

In the meantime, our duo enters the Goldstar Train with the crowd and takes their seats.

"Nep?" Tavvi asks. "What the hell did you spray on the floor?"

"Oh!"

She rummages through her bag and pulls out the bottle again. "It's water from another planet! The water there was just really dense, so it's pretty much like oil. Perfect for getting someone off your trail!"

Tavvi nods before turning his attention to the window. After a few minutes of silence, Tavvi turns back to Neptia.

"Hey!" he says. "Did you notice that one of the officers chasing us had wings?"

Neptia closes her computer compact and looks at Tavvi, confused. "What are you talking about?" she asks.

"Well, one of the officers chasing us - not the one you tripped up; the other one - grew a pair of wings to jump over the water. Did you see the wings?"

Neptia shakes her head, looking concerned. "No, I didn't see any wings."

Tavvi sighs and looks out the window with his chin in his hand.

I swear I saw him grow wings. he thinks to himself.

CHAPTER SEVEN

REPORT ON NOQUT...INCOMING...READY...

Noqut is the fifth planet in the Thria Solar System. Once an uninhabitable ice giant, Noqut's extremely low temperatures made it impossible to populate. Then, seemingly out of nowhere, the sun that Noqut was circling became a red giant, swallowing three planets, - don't worry; they were evacuated. With a much closer sun Noqut soon began to melt, transforming from ice to 95% water.

After some research by the Intergalactic Research and Travel Department, the planet was deemed safe for travel and habitation. Noqut is now a vacation paradise. Despite being composed of mostly water and containing only three hotels, an estimated 74% of the universe has traveled to this ocean planet. An exciting factor that helps visitors enjoy their stay is the special terraforming guns that allow the creation of land masses that must be destroyed at nightfall.

For information about hotels or instructions for using terraforming guns, please contact...

Before the train stops at the station, Neptia recommends they change into something lighter than the coats they are wearing. As they disembark, the duo makes a dash to the station changing rooms. Rifling through their separate bags, Neptia finds a yellow button-up shirt with matching shorts and Tavvi discovers a bunched-up, black polo. Upon exiting the station, they find people sitting, drinking, and chatting on the station's stairway.

"Things are a bit more relaxed here, huh?" Tavvi observes.

"Yeah," Neptia replies. "Keep in mind, we're standing on one of, like...I dunno...seven places that have land that can be removed. They're just enjoying their time here."

They walk down the rest of the stairs only to be met with water gently lapping over the last few steps. Tavvi looks out over the ocean while Neptia calls over a waterbus. The red giant can be seen clearly in the sky but the rest of the planet does not appear to mind. Small and large mounds of land are littered throughout the clear blue water. Each mass is filled with people sunbathing and children playing, as the occasional water surfer or water jet passes by.

"Oh!" Neptia exclaims. "We can relax for a couple of days, the next Goldstar Train won't be here for a bit."

Tavvi turns around and looks at Neptia skeptically.

"Plus, I managed to get us a nice hotel. Without stealing!" she says with a proud smile.

"How?" Tavvi asks.

"Well, I had enough money stowed away. Plus it's a vacation, so why not?"

"This isn't a vacation, Nep. We're supposed to be finding Rialea, remember?"

"Oh, come on," she waves a hand at Tavvi. "It won't hurt for us to take a couple of days off from searching."

Tavvi begins to open his mouth to argue, but the sound of three bell chimes rings out, and the duo looks to the right to see a waterbus pull up.

"Bus's here!" Neptia cries out.

The waterbus stops at the bottom of the station's steps, and Nep and Tavvi join the people crowding in, almost filling up the vehicle. After everyone has entered, the bus driver closes the doors and drives off to a nearby hotel. While on the bus, Tavvi inspects the crowd as Neptia checks her computer compact. There are several different species surrounding them, either taking the bus to a hotel or somewhere else on the planet.

It would be near-impossible to name every being Tavvi can see. There are the Strarn: jelly-like beings whose skeletons can be seen from outside the jelly bodies that protect them. The Teralefts shift around them, their human-like forms mostly covered by leaves that touch their feet and a large flower atop their heads. Last are the Elementals (their true name has yet to be translated, seeing as their language is centuries older than anyone can estimate) who are simple beings composed of a single element mixed with some sort of stone. The water variation is more prevalent here.

As Tavvi looks around, the area briefly dims, beings, people, and man-made islands that were not there seconds earlier flicker into existence. Tavvi blinks and rubs his eyes, the whole area turning gray like an old photograph. Was this from his past? Could this be a clue to finding out who he is?

"Tavvi?"

He turns around to see the white silhouette of the woman from his dreams standing where Neptia was moments before. He rubs his eyes again, and the gray images recede, everything returning to the present. Tavvi is now staring at Neptia, who stares back with a concerned look on her face.

"Are you okay?" she asks.

"Y-yeah," he stammers out. "I'll-I'll tell you when we get to the hotel."

Neptia nods, still slightly worried. After a few minutes, the waterbus stops at a hotel on one of the planet's few natural land masses, and everyone exits, including the duo. As they enter the lobby, Neptia snatches a paper off the wall, ripping up another wanted poster of the stowaways. Tavvi shakes his head at her, trailing behind as Nep checks in.

Once in the room, Tavvi sits on the bed and sighs. "I think I've been here before," he says.

"Really?" Neptia perks up from unpacking her half-empty bag. "I mean it's not surprising seeing as almost everyone's been here at some–"

She freezes and looks at Tavvi directly, realizing they might have a clue. "Do you remember anything? People? Places? Anything at all?!"

Taken aback, Tavvi stumbles over his words. "I mean...I remember coming to this planet with this woman. I couldn't see her face though..."

"Do you think it was your mom? Or an aunt or girlfriend?"

"I-I'm not sure."

She pats his head and smiles. "Don't worry about it. Let's just go out and enjoy the planet for the day, okay?"

Tavvi nods, and they make their way to the door. Next to the hotel is a small city on another land mass, separated only by a bridge and a short walk. Once in the city, Neptia heads straight for a nearby restaurant, leaving Tavvi outside to stare at the ocean.

As he approaches the shore, a perfect sphere of water appears in front of him. He jumps a bit and reaches out to tap the sphere with his index finger. Water trickles down his finger as he breaks the sphere's surface tension. He slowly reaches his cupped hands under the orb, and the ball of water settles down.

"What are you doing?" A voice comes from behind him.

Tavvi shakes his hand, and the sphere turns into liquid, falling into the ocean. He whirls around to find Neptia holding a greasy bag in her right hand.

"N-nothing!" Tavvi stammers out. "Let's eat!"

She sits down in the sand next to him and hands him a styrofoam box.

"I hope you like onion-fried noodles! That's one of the few human foods they serve here!"

Tavvi nods, and they eat in silence.

"I think I wanna go swimming," Neptia says finally.

"You got a swimsuit?" Tavvi asks.

"Nope."

"Neither do I. It doesn't matter. I can't swim anyways."

"Really?"

"Yep."

"Maybe when you get your memories back, I can teach you."

Tavvi shrugs and returns his focus to his food. After they finish, they decide to explore. The little city is filled with small shops and museums about the history of the planet.

A few hours later, the sky begins to darken. Most of the shops have closed and Noqut's police are instructing people to destroy their man-made islands. The duo tiredly walks the short trek back to their hotel room.

Tavvi opens his eyes to find himself on that familiar cliff. He sits up, and rather than the moon coming down in a brilliant explosion of white like last time, the woman is directly in front of him. He stands up and approaches her.

"Let me ask you something," she says.

She waves her hand to her side and five circles appear: moving pictures of a younger Tavvi with the woman by his side in a white silhouette. They're on Noqut - swimming, eating, and playing on a man-made island.

"Do you remember coming to this planet?"

"No," Tavvi replies. "I don't remember anything. I don't even remember what planet I'm from."

The woman nods slightly and flicks the tag on Tavvi's ear with her index finger. The gesture sends a loud, piercing noise through Tavvi's head, causing him to fall to the ground, screaming and holding his head in agony. A smile forms on the woman's face.

"Some of your magic should be coming back to you once you wake," she says. "But your memories must stay hidden for the time being." Her eyes fill with regret. "My apologies."

The cliff explodes, leaving Tavvi floating in total darkness, covering his head in an attempt to keep away the piercing noise traveling through his brain.

After an undetermined amount of time has passed, Tavvi wakes up in the real world again. He rubs the sleep from his eyes and wonders why the ceiling is so close to his face. Looking down, he finds that he is floating in the air. Now wide awake, he lets out a scream and falls to the ground with a loud thud.

The noise wakes Neptia up with a shock and she looks over to find Tavvi on the floor, groaning in pain.

"Tavvi!" she screeches out, rushing to check on him. "Are you okay?! What happened?"

"I-I'm fine," he stammers out, waving his hand in front of him flippantly. "I just fell out of bed."

She nods, still groggy, before climbing back into her bed and turning over. Tavvi manages to stand up and stretch, still groaning slightly. He looks over at a potted plant that is sitting on the table. He focuses on it closely as the plant begins to float above the small table. Astonished, he slowly stretches his hand out in front of him, and the plant begins to float toward his hand.

He focuses harder, and in a flash, the plant zips over in a millisecond and rests in his hand. Tavvi blinks and runs his fingers through his hair with his free hand. He climbs back into the bed and sets the plant in front of him, hugging his knees in distress.

Who the hell am I? he questions himself. *What the hell am I? Am I some sort of circus performer who ended up in the wrong place? Am I a monster or something? Why are all these things happening to me? Why?*

These thoughts continue to flood his brain until he passes out from exhaustion.

Chapter Eight

After another half day of enjoying Noqut, Tavvi and Neptia find themselves back at the station, sneaking onto another Goldstar Train. Once in their seats, Tavvi glances over at Neptia.

"Nep?" Tavvi hesitates.

She turns from the window with a receding view of Noqut and focuses her attention on Tavvi.

"What's your reason for riding the Goldstar Line? I mean, you're pretty much gonna travel through most of the galaxy with no permanent stop! What's the point?"

Neptia looks back out the window and sighs, deep in thought. After a few moments, she answers.

"Well," she begins. "I guess I started riding to get away from my family but to stay close at the same time. Ya know, I was supposed to take over the Goldstar Line at one point, but I didn't want to. So, after a fight with my–"

"Parents, you ran away, and you've been on the train ever since," Tavvi finishes.

"How...how the heck do you know about that?"

Tavvi describes his dream about the figures in the mansion on Viona. Neptia stares blankly and sinks into her seat. As he finishes his story, the train is far into the depths of space.

"That's...that did happen. Exactly," Neptia says, stunned.

They sit in silence for a while, as Neptia redirects her attention out the window again, utterly speechless. Tavvi watches his friend before finally deciding to break the silence.

"You know," he begins. "I'm not sure if we'll ever find that planet. I don't know where we'll go, but if we can't ever find anything, I'd be okay staying with you and traveling the Goldstar Line."

Neptia smiles at him. "I like having you around, too. Plus, now you can keep an extra eye out during long train rides so I can sleep longer!"

"That's all I'm good for?!" Tavvi falls back, clutching his chest in mock pain.

The two friends break into laughter.

Report on Honta...incoming...ready...

Honta is the fourth planet in the Ceccy Solar System. At one point, Honta consisted of an endless white-sanded desert, with no usable resources and no ability to support a population. Then, approximately 3,500 years ago, a meteorite the size of Terra's moon (also known as Earth, for you historians and nobles) collided with the planet, leaving only about 60% of Honta intact. However, rather than becoming one of the millions of meteorite-damaged planets, something strange happened on Honta: hidden among the debris, it began to sprout life.

Lush green plants began to grow and eventually, trees and wildlife appeared! Honta went from a desert to a forest planet in a matter of some-odd hundred years! Testing from the IRTD has proved the planet is safe for travel and habitation, and the universe has flocked to it!

Despite its breathtaking mountains and fantastic wildlife, Honta is mostly used for vacation estates. A recent poll has shown that over 45% of the estates sold or rented on Honta are vacation homes.

For information on estates or mountain tours, please visit...

The Goldstar Train pulls up to the station's platform and the stowaways slip off, hidden among a crowd of people. Neptia immediately recommends a mountain tour. Tavvi hesitates at first, faltering as he confesses his fear of heights, but with Neptia's encouragement, he quickly matches her enthusiasm. However, as they begin to walk to an airship boarding station for the mountain tour, Tavvi's head develops a pounding pain. His vision soon turns into flashbacks similar to the ones he experienced on the waterbus on Honta. He grabs his head and groans out in pain, rocking back on the balls of his feet.

Neptia grabs his shoulders, her voice buzzing in Tavvi's head as she asks him what's wrong. She then seizes his right hand, but before someone can call a paramedic, the two of them shoot into the air like a rocket.

Neptia lets out a high-pitched screech as they fly up and slow to a stop, hovering above the world. Tavvi's headache dulls, and he opens his eyes to find Honta far below him. Panic rises in his chest at the height, but he calms down when he sees his friend. Neptia clings to his right hand, huddled against him and whimpering with her eyes closed shut. Slowly, Tavvi leans down and pushes his free hand in front of him, yanking it back in surprise when he feels solid ground.

He turns back to Neptia and murmurs, "Calm down. It's okay. I'm here."

"O-okay," she stammers out.

"Great," he says calmly. "Now, put one of your feet down."

She nods with her eyes closed and puts her left foot down. Neptia makes a sound of understanding and follows with the right foot. She opens her eyes and looks around the cloudy sky before turning her attention to Tavvi, confused.

"Wha-what the hell?!" she yells. "Are you doing this?!"

"Y-yeah," he answers sheepishly. "I-I'm pretty sure!"

"Well, get us down! Can you?"

"I-I can try, I guess."

He closes his eyes and begins to focus on a mental image of them safely standing on firm ground. Meanwhile, Neptia is gazing around, beginning to question if she is dreaming and will wake up in a hotel somewhere on the planet and–

Oh crap, she just looked down.

She lets out a high-pitched screech and loses her grip on Tavvi's arm, plummeting down to the planet below.

"TAVVI!" she cries out as she falls.

Neptia sobs, the wind whistling through her ears. She gasps for air and is yanked to a stop by Tavvi, who has broken his focus to quickly grab his falling friend. They lock eyes, shock and fear evident on both of their faces.

Neptia barely hesitates before she grabs Tavvi's coat and begins to pull herself up, grunting and straining. She pulls her left foot up to try and climb on his shoulders, but her foot instead meets something like a small step. She looks down at her foot and finds that it's resting on something solid, yet unseen. Pushing up, she moves her right foot ahead and there's another perfect, unseen step waiting for her.

"Um, I know you're probably in shock…" Tavvi says. "But could you please move? You're not that light…"

"Shut up!" Neptia yells. "I'm going!"

She groans and shakes her head, turning to Tavvi's side and holding his arm tight. Eventually, Tavvi focuses his attention on the planet below, and they slowly float down to the ground where they are met by a group of natives and travelers who gasp and move out of the way as they land. Once safely on the ground, they decide to skip the mountain tour, and instead, begin a search for a place to stay in the next town over.

THE TWO FRIENDS WALK in silence, wandering through a town before finding a hotel and checking into a room. After Neptia enters the room, she closes the door, turns around to Tavvi, takes a deep breath, and…

"What the hell was that?!" Neptia yells out.

"I don't know!" Tavvi yells back. "First thing, I'm seeing flashbacks, next thing you know, I'm shooting up in the air!"

"Do you think the flashbacks could be related to you doing…whatever that was?"

"I don't know." He falls back on the bed and looks out the large picture window. "It could be. Or hell, maybe that woman on the cliff did this."

"Woman on the cliff?" Neptia tilts her head slightly in confusion. "What are you talking about?"

"Well, ever since Lethum, I've been having these dreams with this lady on a cliff…" He gives an abridged version of the dreams.

Neptia puts her hand on her chin as she walks over to the small couch and sits down. "Have you ever met this woman before?" she asks. "You know, before you lost your memories?"

Tavvi sits back up and shakes his head. "I don't know."

Neptia stands up and huffs in frustration, pacing around the room. "There *has* to be a connection with your dreams, the flashbacks, and finding Rialea! I know there has to be!"

Tavvi shrugs and looks down at the floor. "You know…after everything - the dreams, flashbacks, and floating in the air…I 'm not sure we'll ever find Rialea. Hell, I don't think I wanna keep looking. Just too many dead ends and–"

A slap from Neptia makes contact with his right cheek. He grabs the injury and inhales sharply as Neptia stares down at him with anger.

"Finding Rialea is the point of this adventure. Not giving up!" She grabs his shoulders, forcing him to look directly at her. "We're going to find Rialea and the Nylat System whether you want to or not! And if you don't want to tag along, I'll gladly leave you behind and continue traveling by myself, and I'll find it! I've been alone all this time. Being alone any longer won't hurt me one bit!"

She pushes Tavvi back, stomps to the bathroom, and slams the door. Tavvi lays back on the bed and covers his eyes with his hands as the shower turns on with a whoosh.

Maybe I'd be better at running away from the station police by myself, he thinks to himself.

He looks at the door and considers leaving. *If I leave right now, I can find a cheap house here on the planet, lay low for a bit, and then hop on another train. Then I can just...*

He slaps his forehead and groans. *Okay, I'm being dumb. What the fuck am I even thinking?*

"...AND THEN THEY BOTH fell back to the planet and ran away! I swear on my life!"

Ray and Verla look at the Honta native skeptically. Two hours after Neptia and Tavvi shot up into the sky, Ray and

Verla were sent to Honta with reports of individuals that matched the description of the two stowaways.

"This has to be some kind of prank from HQ, right?" Verla whispers to Ray. "Should we be talking to someone like this at all? Because they seem delusional."

"I hate to say this, " Ray replies. "but I think you're right."

He turns his attention to the native and puts both of his hands in front of him. "Listen, we understand that this is very confusing and possibly scary for you to witness, but if you see anything else weird, call the planet's police, okay? Okay."

He begins to stalk off in the direction of the station, but the native has more to say.

"One of the floating travelers had a tag in his ear!!"

Ray stops and turns back around. "What was that?"

"O-one of them had a tag in his ear. A green and brown one! And the girl he was with had green eyes and dark skin! The man was wearing a gray coat and the girl had a tan one! They looked like the people in those wanted posters!"

Ray smirks, and Verla rolls her eyes in distaste at his smugness.

"Do you know which direction they went?" Ray asks.

The native points down the road leading to the next town over, and Ray thanks them for their time. The officers begin the walk down the road, Ray in front and Verla straggling behind. Verla huffs to herself, wondering if they are on yet another goose chase.

CHAPTER NINE

Tavvi wakes up to find himself in the mansion from his earlier dream about Neptia. The rooms around him echo with the sound of people yelling as shadows dart back and forth frantically. Most of what he can hear amongst the panic is the faint recurring cry of "She's not here! She's not here! She's not..." Eventually, two familiar parental-shaped figures can be recognized among the crowd. They stand with their arms crossed.

"I knew this would happen." A man's voice echoes throughout the room. "Now what?"

"I'm thinking," the woman retorts, frustrated.

The figure of Neptia's mother places a hand on her chin in thought as another figure runs up to them, panting.

"She-she's gone!" A voice gasps out in panicked disbelief, struggling for air as though its owner had just run a marathon. "We've searched every part of this mansion. There is no sign of her anywhere!"

"I see…" The woman replies thoughtfully. The female figure flickers across the wall and sighs. "I suppose we'll have to file a missing person's report."

The panicked figure nods in understanding and begins to leave.

"WAIT!"

The departing shadow freezes, as does every other silhouette in Tavvi's field of vision.

"I also want a press conference, and the reward will be massive!"

"What are you thinking?" Neptia's father asks.

The woman's shadow turns toward the man, and Tavvi can barely make out a smile on her flickering face. "Five million, all across the board."

The man jumps back in astonishment and questions if that would be a practical decision.

The woman lets out a laugh. "Of course! It's only a small chunk of our fortune! And besides…" The woman's figure walks toward a massive stairwell and begins her ascent, the man and several other figures following behind. "The bigger the reward, the more likely someone will bring her home. Whether she wants to come or not."

Tavvi's eyes flutter open. He props his upper body up on his elbows to find Neptia on the couch across from him, sound asleep. As Tavvi watches, she opens one eye, then the other, and sits up, rubbing her face.

"Hey," Tavvi says timidly. "Thank you for not leaving me like you said you might."

Neptia shakes her head at him. "Don't worry about it," she says. "I was just angry and confused after yesterday, and besides, I would have been lonely without you."

Tavvi gives her a small smile and she returns it.

"Anyways," Neptia says, lying back down. "Let's go back to sleep. I wanna get some breakfast and explore this planet before we have to go tomorrow."

Tavvi nods and lays his head back down, relief flooding his body.

AFTER A QUICK BREAKFAST the following morning, the duo sets out to wander the surrounding city. They are lodging in one of the smaller towns on the planet, so there isn't much to see, but Neptia does manage to find a dancing flower at a small shop to commemorate her visit. However, after a few hours of boredom, Neptia insists they should try a mountain tour again, and Tavvi acquiesces reluctantly.

"I think we should ask around to see if there's a closer tour station so we don't have to go back to where those people saw us floating," Neptia says as she scans their surroundings.

"Yeah, maybe," Tavvi agrees absentmindedly as something catches his eye.

His gaze hesitates on a woman cloaked in the same gray coat as he is currently wearing. He follows her with his eyes as she walks away from a shop and shakes her head, flipping her long hair back to expose–

A tag on her ear. A tag like his.

She walks off in the opposite direction, and Neptia tries to follow Tavvi's eyes, obviously not noticing anything unusual.

"Nep, you can go without me," he says, before chasing after the woman.

Extremely confused and irritated at being abandoned, she shouts in frustration, "Hey, what the hell?!"

Sensing movement in the corner of her eye, she glances over to see Ray and Verla walking toward her.

Fucking shit! She groans and begins to walk at a decently fast pace in the opposite direction, hoping to find a crowd to disappear into.

"She's trying to get away," Verla says under her breath.

"I can see that," Ray says, trying to match Neptia's speed.

He can't chase her without attracting the attention of the locals. The people here are too curious and desperate for any form of entertainment and will only slow him down.

"Go find the other one."

"I really don't think that's a good idea, because if there are two of us–"

Her protest is cut short when she realizes that Ray has left her side in pursuit of Neptia.

Neptia's pursuer is right behind her. After every attempt to shake him, she looks back to find he has not lost any momentum.

I can't circle around any blocks, she says to herself, still walking as fast as possible. *Shaking him won't work like that. Running is out of the question. If I attract any attention, he has nothing to lose, and he's more than likely faster than me. Dammit!*

As she mulls over her options for escape, she glances to her left to see a hotel. A sign hanging on the front door reads, "Hotel Miracova".

This is gonna be a bit risky, but it's worth a shot!

She darts into the hotel with Ray right behind her. The interior is decorated with marbled white and pink walls and a marble-white floor. Neptia turns down a hallway, making a straight line for the stairs as Ray follows with his hands behind his back as though he is out for a leisurely stroll. They walk up to the third floor and down a long hallway. Neptia continually checks behind her, only to find Ray in hot pursuit.

Ray's expression is one of determination with a hint of a smile. Neptia takes a deep breath and works up to a sprint. Surprised, Ray mimics the girl's actions, chasing her down the hallway as he yells at her to freeze. Seeing an open door up ahead, Neptia slows down and dashes inside a room.

Is that where the other stowaway is? Ray asks himself. *Two for one!*

He races into the hotel room in time to see Neptia step up onto the windowsill in front of an open window on the other side of the room.

Ray lunges at her, hands outstretched. His grin is gone, replaced by a look of concern.

"NO!!" he yells.

Before he can grab the back of her jacket, she flings herself forward. The officer shoves his head through the window and looks down. The gaudy "Hotel Miracova" sign on the front of the building blocks his view of the ground below. Ray pulls his head inside and puts his hands on his face, screaming in frustration, before pulling out his computer compact.

"This is Ray," he says, slightly aggravated and out of breath. "I need any and all available officers on scene at Hotel Miracova for a search. Neptia Goldstar was spotted, but I can't find her after she jumped out of a window."

Ray paces between the window and the bed, still relating details to the person on the other end of the line. Meanwhile, Neptia hangs from the first "a" of Miracova. She looks down and exhales slowly before releasing her grip and bracing herself as she falls one story to the ground below.

Where the hell did Tavvi run off to?! she thinks to herself while ducking into an alleyway. She tries to stay low and out of view of any nearby reinforcements as she begins the search for her friend.

CHAPTER TEN

MEANWHILE, TAVVI FOLLOWS THE girl with the tag across the city. Occasionally, she glances back as if sensing someone behind her, but Tavvi quickly ducks into a crowd or behind a lamppost until the girl continues on her way. Eventually, she leads him to an alleyway. Tavvi peaks around a building and watches as the girl enters the alley and stops at a door. She looks to her left and right once before closing her eyes and slightly hanging her head.

"*Release,*" the woman murmurs.

The tag on her ear pops off in her hand and she presses it to a scanner on the right of the door. Tavvi lets out a gasp and his eyes widen in surprise as the door opens. After she walks through the entrance, Tavvi dashes to the door, excited.

"Release!" he orders, placing his hand over his tag.

The tag does not move.

"Release!"

Nothing.

"Release!"

No reaction.

Realizing that this is not going to work, he awkwardly crouches in front of the scanner, tilting his head to place his tag in front of it. With a small click, the door swings wide open, revealing a pitch-black abyss with no discernable features except for a straight white line that emits a soft glow as it zigzags out into the void. Taking a deep breath, Tavvi steps onto the white line and begins tracing its path.

As the door swings shut behind him, his surroundings are completely black except for the white line branching out, resembling tree branches in winter. As Tavvi observes his environment, the line leads him to an open door. Swallowing his fear, he walks over the threshold. He squints as his eyes adjust to the dim light, stumbling into a room filled with brown leather suitcases arranged and hanging upright from the ceiling in a circular shape. The luggage sits lifeless and stiff, reminding Tavvi of an auditorium filled with empty seats.

Out of curiosity, he decides to see what is inside. Upon lifting one, he finds that it is surprisingly heavy, almost as though it contains rocks. He lowers it to the ground and slowly clicks the latches open. Tavvi then leans back slightly in preparation as he lifts the flap open and–

There's a person inside, huddled in the fetal position with the exact same tag as his. The only difference is this person's tag is open wide and wires stretch out of it, tendrilling out where they attach to the suitcase.

Tavvi covers his mouth and shoves himself away from the bag, unable to scream or even think a single coherent thought. He looks around and makes the grim realization that the other briefcases must be filled with people, too. He reaches up, running his thumb over his own tag and feeling a seam on its side. He tries to pry it open, but as he does, he is flooded with memories of standing in a room just like this one. He sees himself exiting the Greencoal Train, prior to boarding the Goldstar.

"...and then I said, 'it can't be that much, cuz it was a hand-me-down!'"

"That's ridiculous. I'm glad you had some sense."

Tavvi snaps out of his trance at the sound of two voices. He looks around for a hiding place and quickly dives into the shadows in the corner. Two humans enter the room, cloaked in white lab coats, black gloves, and medical masks. They immediately focus on the bag on the ground.

"Looks like *someone* didn't hang this up correctly!" one huffs out, closing it and hanging it back up on its hook.

"Fuck you!" the other replies. "I hung it up fine! Anyways, how many do we need?"

"Two."

They each grab a suitcase and walk out of the room, their footsteps fading in the distance. Once the room falls silent, Tavvi runs out the door, searching for an exit from this strange place. Retracing his path, he finally finds the door he came in and charges out of it shoulder first. Crashing onto the pavement outside, he grabs his head and gasps for air, his eyes wide.

"NEPTIAAA!!" he yells out.

MEANWHILE, NEPTIA TRAVERSES THE city, simultaneously trying to avoid officers and find Tavvi before he gets himself into too much trouble.

"...Tiaaaaa!!"

She whips around, attempting to puzzle out where that familiar voice came from.

"NEPTIAAAA!!"

She turns to see Tavvi barreling toward her.

"Tavvi!" she exhales in relief. "Where have you—"

Her sentence is cut short as she is tackled in a hug. Neptia struggles to keep her balance as Tavvi screams into her chest, sobbing.

"I-Nep-there's-I-I-think..." Tavvi blubbers out.

Neptia looks around for any sign of danger and rubs his head in reassurance

"Hey. Look, it's okay," she murmurs in her most calming voice. "What's wrong? Take some deep breaths and let's talk, okay?"

Eventually, Tavvi calms down and releases his grip on Neptia.

"I need to show you something." His voice is barely above a whisper.

Neptia surveys their surroundings and raises an eyebrow at Tavvi.

"Now, like... now? First, I think we need to get off the planet because–"

"No, Nep. Now. It has to do with me getting my memories back."

"What?! Well, what are we waiting for?! Let's go! Lead the way!"

Tavvi guides her to the alleyway he ran from only minutes before. There is no way Neptia will believe what he has seen without proof. They pause in front of the door.

"Is there someone in there that knows you or something?" Neptia asks.

Tavvi just holds up a finger to silence her and groans as he awkwardly crouches by the scanner once again. Neptia lets out a little giggle, but her full attention soon turns to the door as it swings open to the black void of a room, the single white line glowing eerily. Neptia stands in awe as Tavvi steps inside, motioning for her to follow.

"Tavvi…" Neptia sounds scared. "What is this?"

"Don't worry," he replies, holding his hand out. "I'll keep you safe. You just have to come inside,"

Neptia squints and reaches her hand into the room, past Tavvi. After taking a deep breath, she finally steps through the entrance. Tavvi finds his hand in a death grip, Neptia pressed as close to him as she can get.

"Tavvi!" Neptia whispers as they begin walking. "Do you remember ever being here before? Or anywhere like this?"

"Yeah," he replies. "Something like that."

Tavvi's attention turns to an open door, and he leads the way into the room, the familiar sight of infinite suitcases looming over them.

"I'm going to show you what's inside these cases," he begins hesitantly. "Do you want to see?"

Neptia nods and swallows.

"Y-yeah!" she says, sounding almost nervous. "I've seen a lot of messed up stuff while I've been traveling, there's nothing that you can show me that can–"

Just as she is almost done talking, Tavvi taps her arm and Neptia looks down to see what has already been ingrained in her friend's mind.

She stands frozen in fear.

"What the fuck?!"

Neptia stumbles and almost falls backward, but luckily, Tavvi catches her. He hugs her in a vain attempt to try and calm her down from her state of shock. However, not even a minute later, she kicks herself out of Tavvi's grasp and finds her footing, standing up and pointing at the suitcase.

"T-Tavvi...!" she stammers out, still pointing. "Th-this is... Oh, my fucking god, we need to go to the police! We need to tell someone! Maybe the military or–"

"HEY!"

They turn their attention to find a man in a lab coat and medical mask standing in the doorway.

"Who the fuck are you two?! And-"

His sentence is cut short as Neptia throws what appears to be a mini booklet at the man.

"RUN!" Tavvi shrieks.

They charge in the opposite direction, exiting out another door and sprinting down a dark hallway. Tavvi quickly realizes they have no idea where they are going. He tries to bring this to Neptia's attention, but she shakes him off and points to an open door farther ahead. The duo finally reaches the door and barges through it only to find–

They're on another planet.

They look around and find that they are no longer on Honta. On this particular planet, it is already dusk. Unlike Honta's clean, modern, and developed world, their surroundings resemble a jungle, with vines and various other plant life covering the few buildings that can be seen in the distance.

The door swings shut behind them, and they walk forward to find that their exit sits on the cliff of an overgrown building. Confused, Neptia pulls out her computer compact and conducts a search.

"It looks like...we're not on Honta anymore. We're on a planet called...'Sphe.'"

CHAPTER ELEVEN

"...Sphe is the fourth planet in the...It's not by Rialea, so we don't care. Sphe is mostly composed of jungles with spruce cities located around the planet. It's also known for being the hub of the Semifuse trafficking line, so travelers should be extremely cautious when wandering the planet."

"Wait, wait," Tavvi cuts in. "The what?"

Neptia scrolls up.

"It's a human trafficking line that's–"

She stops reading and looks at Tavvi, slightly concerned.

"T-Tavvi?" she stammers out. "The person in the suitcase. He had a tag like you. Do...do you think you've been trafficked?"

"I don't know!" Tavvi groans. "I don't remember anything other than...waking up in that black and white area and...oh ..."

"Tavvi...I think you might have been trafficked."

Tavvi stands frozen in disbelief at this statement, but he eventually comes to terms with it, falling on his knees and looking out at the jungle planet spread before him. Neptia frowns down at his broken figure, wearing a look of concern.

"Why?"

It's the only thing he's able to say. Neptia puts her hands in her pockets and shakes her head, looking down.

"You might have just been at the wrong place at the wrong time," she offers, sitting next to Tavvi. "Or the planet you lived on was a shitshow and you had to leave it any way you knew how. There are a lot of reasons."

They sit in solemn silence, surveying the world before them as the sound of various species rustling through the trees echoes through the sky. Soon, however, the quiet comfort is broken by the sound of some voices in the distance.

"C'mon." Neptia stands up and offers Tavvi her hand. "Let's get down from here and find a place to ride out the night. We'll worry about our stuff later."

Covered in plant life, they find a nearby town and a hotel with rooms for rent. The moment they enter their room, Tavvi plops down on the couch, and Neptia settles on the bed in front of him.

"Are you okay?" she asks quietly, studying Tavvi who is still in a state of shock.

"Yeah, I think so," he mumbles.

He takes a deep breath and looks at Neptia, smiling slightly.

"If I don't get my memories back, at least we'll never have to find out how I ended up in the Semifuse line in the first place!"

Neptia smiles back and nods.

"I think we should try and get back to Honta from that...place. I don't know how many trains make it out to an area like this. It'll be the easiest way, I think."

"I dunno," Tavvi says, putting his hand on his chin. "We don't have a map of the place, and we might just end up on another planet, further away from our goal. Plus, the area will be on high alert after us being in there, and we might get caught, and who knows what'll happen then."

"I hate to say this, but you're right."

Neptia pulls out her computer compact and flips it open.

"I think the only option here is to just wait for another Goldstar Train, which won't be for another three days. Might as well just stay here and get some more clues about Rialea."

Tavvi nods in agreement.

"Yeah, there's no point in leaving just yet when there's a possible connection to my past here."

Neptia gets up and walks over to the sofa at the far end of the room, gesturing for Tavvi to take the bed.

"Right," she says. "We'll stay here until the next Goldstar Train shows up. We'll go back to Honta to get our bags. While we're here, we'll get more clues and answers."

She removes the cushions and pulls out the mattress from inside the couch before turning her attention back to Tavvi.

"Was there anything in your bag that you really needed? Medicine? Anything at all?"

Tavvi shakes his head as Neptia takes off her shoes and lays back on the mattress.

"Also, while you were chasing that girl, one of the officers - the guy with black hair who chased us at the station - found me and chased me around the city."

"Wait, what?!"

"I was gonna tell you earlier, but you took me off to that briefcase place and I forgot!"

"How the hell did you get away?!"

"Oh! I kinda made him think that I jumped out a window, but I hung onto the sign outside of the hotel until he got away from the windowsill."

Tavvi groans and rubs his face in response while moving to the bed.

"That's probably the least crazy thing I've done to get away from the police if it makes you feel any better. One time, I rigged my bags to a door and when anyone opened it, it would swing and hit them."

"Nice story. I'm going to bed."

Tavvi opens his eyes to see the shining white woman watching him. He can instantly tell that he is dreaming.

"How close?" he asks of the woman. "How close am I to finding out who I am?"

"Only time will only tell," she murmurs. "Though, you may–"

Her speech is cut off by something in the cave behind them. Tavvi sits up to get a better look. A figure comes into view as it approaches them from the depths.

It's Neptia. Holding her head and groaning.

Tavvi's eyes open wide in shock, but an amused smile grows on the woman's face. Neptia rubs her face and looks up in shock upon seeing Tavvi and the woman.

"T-Tavvi?!" she gasps, her voice echoing into the cave. "Wha-what are you doing here, and who is that?!"

Before Tavvi can answer, the woman walks past Tavvi and cups Neptia's face in her hands. Neptia jerks her head back and steps away in defense. The woman's smile grows.

"You are a very valuable thing in this universe," the woman whispers.

She then walks to the edge of the cliff, glancing back at the shocked duo.

"I can't wait to meet both of you. You have made my life *much* easier."

Tavvi stands and runs to the woman, but before he can, the cliff explodes, and he wakes up with a shock. Over on the sofa, he can hear Neptia gasping for air. As they collect themselves, they sit up and lock eyes, breathing hard and trying to wrap their minds around the dream they just shared.

"Tavvi..." Neptia breathes out. "A-are those the dreams that you've been having?"

Tavvi simply nods and cups his face in his hands.

"I-is that how you found out about me?"

"I saw the fight you had with your parents, you running away, and the aftermath of the night you left. I saw...her...floating by me after you ran away."

"How the hell could she even know about me?!" Neptia yells out. "I've never met her before! Hell, she probably doesn't even know me!"

Tavvi shakes his head in response, unsure. Neptia blinks and hugs her knees.

"I realize I've been asking a lot of things about you, and you don't know the answers to those questions. I'm sorry."

Tavvi gets out of bed and pats Neptia's head, causing her to look up at him.

"It's fine," he says with a smile.

He walks past her and heads for the shower in an attempt to quiet his racing mind. As he closes the door to the bathroom, Neptia begins to think she has made a huge mistake letting Tavvi tag along with her.

She has been to places and seen things that no one should ever see in their life. Sharing dreams with someone she hardly knows. People in suitcases. It is all too much. Neptia hides her head in her knees with the thought of seeing another human - no, another being - in a suitcase like that! She hears the water running in the shower and glances at the bathroom door.

She figures she can make a break for it while he is in there. Just grab her coat, and she will be alone again and can forget everything that happened. It's a perfect plan!

Tavvi has regained more of his magic powers. Waving his hands, he turns the hot water streaming down from the showerhead into a stream of ice, freezing and unfreezing it in its place. He makes soap bottles float around him and accidentally throws a bottle of shampoo at the ceiling, causing it to break. He gasps. He was able to do all this with a flick of the wrist and a few words like "float" and "freeze." Quickly finishing his shower, he turns the faucet off, admiring a sphere of water he has managed to capture in his hand.

Nep has got to see this! he thinks to himself.

He gently puts the sphere down and changes into his shirt and pants before picking the sphere back up and entering the main room.

"Hey Nep, check this–"

He stops mid-sentence at the sight of Neptia with her coat on and her right hand on the doorknob. She snaps around to look at him, her eyes full of tears.

"Oh... you finished your shower."

CHAPTER TWELVE

Tavvi looks at Neptia, unblinking, as she drops her hand off the doorknob and walks over to sit on the end of the bed, covering her face. Tavvi sets his sphere on the table next to the bed and sits beside her.

"Nep, what were you–"

"Trying to leave," she mumbles from behind her hands.

"Why?"

"I'm tired of this!"

She moves her hands to her lap and begins crying hard.

"I-I thought that you tagging along would make my life less lonely but it just made it worse! You saw my personal life, and I saw a human being in a suitcase! I didn't want to see that! I didn't want any of this!

"I didn't have a purpose for running or riding the Goldstar Line! I thought we could find out who you were and where you came from! I didn't expect–"

Neptia's sobbing rant is cut off by Tavvi hugging her.

"I'm sorry," Tavvi says quietly. "I didn't know we'd be going through all of this–"

"No shit, you didn't!" Neptia replies, pushing him off. "You don't even know your real name!"

Tavvi lets out a sigh and runs his fingers through his hair.

"Nep, let me just say this. If you want to leave, you can go."

Neptia opens her eyes wide at Tavvi who is staring at the wall across from them.

"I understand that what you've seen has put you on edge and has made you scared to be around me. Now, I don't know what'll happen if we keep looking for Rialea, but if you don't feel up to it - especially seeing as you're one of the most wanted people in the galaxy right now - you are free to leave right now, and I won't stop you."

Neptia studies him in silence as Tavvi continues to avert his gaze to the wall.

"You can leave whenever you choose to, and I won't be upset or mad at you. I don't want you to worry about me. I'll be fine. I promise."

Neptia stands up and walks away from Tavvi, sitting on the end of the sofa's mattress. She rubs her face and takes her coat off before curling up on it.

"Can you...stop looking at me, please?" she asks.

Tavvi nods and grabs the sphere, returning to the bathroom where he sends the orb down the drain. After shaking off the remnants of water left on his hands, he locks eyes with his reflection in the mirror and glares at himself.

Who the fuck are *you?* he scolds himself. *Why...no,* how *did you end up in this situation, you dumbass?!*

He hits his hand on the sink and rests his head in between his arms. He begins to consider what would happen if Neptia decides to leave him for good. After all, he did say she could leave whenever she wanted to. He figures he can scrounge through station lockers and sell items and fake tickets like Neptia showed him.

But if she abandons him, what will he do about the loneliness? That would be the worst part: being alone and running from station police again. And if Neptia leaves, would he even have to worry about finding Rialea? Deep down he knows that it is crucial to find out who he is, but does he even need to after Neptia leaves? It doesn't matter who he is. Once she is gone, he can just go back to wandering the galaxy alone.

Pulling himself out of his downward spiral, he turns on the faucet to splash some warm water on his face.

Look, she's not gone yet, you idiot, he scolds himself. *I'll think over my plans* if *and* when *she leaves. For now, let's just go to bed.*

He dries his face off and walks back into the main room to find Neptia passed out on the mattress, her left arm covering her face. He lets out a deep sigh and scratches the back of his neck, watching her body rise and fall with each breath before returning to his bed. Once wrapped up in blankets, he pulls the covers over his head in a vain attempt to try and sleep without looking at her.

He wakes up almost every hour to see if Neptia is still across from him. She always is.

Some hours later, after a quick shower and a meal, the two of them leave the hotel to wander the streets and ask around the planet for Rialea's whereabouts. During the walk, Tavvi looks over at Neptia, her eyes red as though she has been crying all night. He hesitantly asks if she is alright.

"Yeah. I'm fine," she snaps. "I'm still really tired."

"Is it because of last night?" he asks.

She just nods and sighs.

"This planet's really small." Tavvi changes the subject. "There's another city across this part of the jungle."

They follow a pathway into the jungle, and Neptia begins to smile at the sounds of life around them. The gentle breeze rustling the leaves, the occasional call from the native birds, and the crunching of branches and leaves under their feet makes Neptia feel a little better.

"You know the offer's still open–"

"I know, Tavvi. Let me just enjoy the sounds around us, please. It's been a while since I've been to a jungle planet."

Tavvi nods and walks by Neptia's side, careful not to encroach in her space. Even he has to admit it is nice to be in such a remote area with no chatter and swarming–

Tavvi stops mid-thought and turns around. He hears murmurs somewhere in the forest. Neptia opens her mouth to speak, but before she can, Tavvi covers her mouth and drags her into the bushes. He releases Neptia and raises his pointer finger to his lip, closing his eyes.

He has managed to catch sight of Ray and Verla through the bushes, carrying on a conversation. Tavvi's eyes open wide in fear, but the officers don't appear to have spotted them yet, and he quickly closes his eyes again like a child playing hide-and-seek.

"...You know, I think you might be onto something here, Ray," Verla says, looking around. "I can see why they might be here. This is a pretty popular smuggling site. And he might be returning to his suitcases or whatever."

"That's one reason I'm glad the station stuck us out here," Ray replies. "The other is that if Neptia Goldstar is here, we can nab her, too! Two for the price of one!"

Verla rolls her eyes at Ray's mention of Neptia. They walk through the jungle a bit more before Verla looks over at Ray.

"Hey, do you think it's possible Neptia's part of the smuggling ring?" Verla asks. "I mean, there's no way she would just be hanging out with a stowaway like him for no good reason."

"It could be," Ray agrees, pulling out his computer compact. "After she ran away from home, she needed food and a place to stay, so what better opportunity for her to get that than smuggling? Easy and a lot of money!"

Great theory dumbasses, Tavvi said to himself in the bushes. *Too bad it's wrong.*

He turns his attention to Neptia.

"Nep, those two officers are here." His voice is so quiet it cannot even be considered a whisper.

She nods and lets out a whimper, causing Tavvi to cover her mouth again. He decides he needs to take charge.

"Okay, here's what I'm going to do. I'm going to run ahead and try to give you a window where you can run away, because they're most likely going to chase after you. I don't know where we're going, but make sure to get the hell out of here, okay?"

Neptia looks at Tavvi and nods before hugging him and whispering in his ear to be careful. He smiles at the message, stands to dust himself off and sprints away.

"...but I mean, what's the motive behind that? It isn't like–"

Ray holds his hand up to silence Verla mid-sentence and closes his eyes. He can hear someone charging through the undergrowth and finally catches a glimpse of Tavvi through the bushes.

"The stowaway is here," Ray says, smiling with something that looks like glee. "Go back to the station and call for back-up."

"Ray, no," she argues. "I think I should stay with you just in case he's armed or whatever. We don't know if he has anything that can hurt–"

She blinks and finds that Ray is no longer in sight. Groaning in frustration, she grabs her head.

"Ray, I'm gonna beat your ass the next time I see you!" she yells out, turning in the direction of the station.

Tavvi dashes through the forest, the wind brushing his face and hands. He knows he must keep running, even if he feels like he is going to keel over any second. He needs to run to keep himself, and more importantly, Neptia safe. He looks around to see he has managed to end up in an abandoned city of sorts.

He dashes past the skeletons of terraformed buildings and soon leaves the crumbling city behind. However, as he continues running, he sees something like a small brick house through the foliage in the distance. With no better idea, he runs toward it, his feet soon hitting cobblestone instead of the soft plants and dirt he has come to expect. Unable to catch sight of any pursuers, Tavvi stops to catch his breath beside a small red brick building composed of four windowless walls and a decrepit roof.

He walks over to the door to find the doorknob rusted shut. As he goes to grab it, the metal crumbles to pieces in his hand. Pushing the door open, he finds nothing but a black void with a white line stretching into the distance, just like the alley entrance on Honta. He contemplates his next steps. Does he risk running inside, ending up somewhere farther away from Neptia, or does he keep running until he can reach a station or some other means of escape? A distant shout makes Tavvi's decision for him.

He steps into the darkness and carefully traces the white pathway created by the line. As he walks, he looks for another door or exit that could lead him and whoever is chasing him to another planet, somewhere far away from Neptia. He begins to panic, wondering if he will ever find Neptia again. He does not want to just go back to wandering aimlessly.

Tavvi shakes the idea out of his head and focuses his thoughts on hoping that Neptia has managed to get somewhere safe, far away from this planet and their pursuers. His thoughts are interrupted by the sight of a door just a little farther ahead. Hurrying toward it, he can feel relief build in his chest until a loud thud is heard somewhere in the distance. He runs now and dodges into the room to try and hide. The room is filled with the familiar sights of suitcases, many of them piled on the floor. He scowls and hides among a pile of them, trying his best to curl into a ball to minimize how easily someone could spot him.

Destroying the bleak quiet of the room, people enter, and Tavvi trembles amid the sounds of heavy footsteps, yelling, and suitcase zippers gliding open and shut. Peeking out behind his hiding spot, Tavvi catches sight of Ray entering the room. He covers his mouth in an attempt to hide further.

"It's okay!" Ray yells out. "I know you're scared, and I'm here to help you!"

Tavvi slowly lowers his hand and looks out at Ray. The workers in the room stare at the officer, irritated. They do not seem concerned to find station police in their trafficking rooms.

"If you come out right now, we can help you find where you come from and get you back to your family. But only if you cooperate and come out now!"

Tavvi studies the officer as Ray repeats his message, turning his head so his words fill the room. After a few minutes, Ray shrugs and continues out the door, several workers filing out after him. Tavvi pokes his head out from behind a piece of luggage and glances around to make sure the coast is clear. After he can safely determine that Ray is gone, he steps out into the open and walks toward the door. He almost makes it to the exit before he feels a strong grip on his right arm.

Snapping his attention to his right, he discovers Ray with a wicked grin on his face and his hand clamped around Tavvi's biceps.

"Gotcha!" Ray sings out.

Chapter Thirteen

"So, what were you doing riding the Goldstar Line with no ticket or pass?" Verla asks Tavvi, who is sitting at a small rectangular table across from her.

After Tavvi was caught by Ray, he was promptly carted off to a small police station located in Sphe's train station. The entrance to the police station has elegant yellow walls and a white marble floor. The ceiling above is adorned with multiple fans. However, the interrogation box - where Tavvi is held captive - is simply a small plain, white cell with two white, plastic chairs and a matching table.

Verla watches the prisoner carefully. From among her colleagues, she was chosen to interrogate Tavvi and attempt to get a statement before the higher-ups decide what to do with him.

"I don't know," Tavvi says.

"Okay. You know there were reports of you riding with Neptia Goldstar, right? *The* Neptia Goldstar. How do you know her?"

"I don't know. I'm sorry,"

Verla shakes her head and turns her attention to her notepad, scribbling something down.

"Was that the real Neptia Goldstar or–"

A knock on the door stops Verla mid-sentence. Both the prisoner and interrogator look up in surprise as Ray pokes his head through the crack in the door. "Verla," Ray says stiffly. "Tap out. You're needed at the navigation desk to look at some footage."

She shrugs and gets up, nodding in acknowledgment as she passes Ray. He takes her place, picking up the notepad she left on the table to continue with the barrage of questions. After a moment, however, he takes off his uniform hat and lets out a sigh as he looks directly at Tavvi.

"We're from the same solar system," Ray says calmly.

Tavvi's eyes widen in surprise as he attempts to passively stare back at Ray.

"How do you know?" Tavvi finally asks.

"The tag in your ear. That's one way, of course."

"Prove it."

Tavvi glares at Ray, and the officer lets out a heavy sigh in response. Ray holds his index and middle finger up together and a small white flame appears above his digits. Either by response or instinct, Tavvi repeats the motion and the same flame appears over his own fingers.

"Told you." Ray says, dropping his hand.

Tavvi copies the motion and looks at Ray, dumbfounded. He takes a deep breath and a small feeling of trust enters Tavvi.

"So that's why I was the only one to see your wings when you were chasing us in Viona's station," Tavvi realizes.

"Huh?" Ray grunts. "Oh! No, no. Everyone can see those. I guess my partner and Little Miss Goldstar were so busy running around to even notice!"

"Ah, I see."

"Anyway," Ray entwines his hands and rests them in front of Tavvi. "I just want to say this, and I don't want to shock you, but you're the product of a–"

"Smuggling ring. I know that."

"Okay, good. Now, my next problem is that I know you don't have your memories, but do you know or remember anything about your home, or hell, even your planet? Because if you remember *anything* that helps us at all, you might be acquitted of all your charges."

Tavvi looks down for a second before looking back up at Ray and shaking his head.

"I don't remember anything," Tavvi says quietly. "I know that I was possibly smuggled, but that's all I know."

"And how do you know Neptia? I mean, if that *is* the real Neptia, because we've had a couple of fakes."

"Neptia saw me after I boarded a Goldstar Train. I never knew who she was, really."

Ray scribbles something down on the notepad, and begins to ask another question, but is stopped by a knock at the door. Verla pokes her head in and studies the two, with Ray looking slightly taken aback.

"Verla, what's going on?" Ray clears his throat.

"Oh, he's free to go, that's all."

Ray jumps out of his seat with a loud "What?!" but Verla holds a hand to his face to quickly shut him up.

"Well, two reasons" she replies in response to his expression. "1) he's been bailed out. And 2) he's gained amnesty on like...twenty-five planets including this one thanks to him leading us right to that smuggling station! So, he can go when he's ready!"

Ray groans and glares at Verla who is wearing a smile. He trudged over to Tavvi and pulled him to his feet, removing the handcuffs. Verla offers to show him to the train station and Tavvi hesitantly accepts.

"HEY!" Ray yells out.

They both turn around as Ray puts his hat on as threateningly as one can.

"I've got my eye on you."

Tavvi blinks and Verla shakes her head, chuckling to herself. After being led through the yellow police station to the exit, Tavvi finds himself back in the bustling train station. He takes a couple of steps away from the police station's entrance to collect himself before heading for the main exit. Pushing through crowds, he has almost reached the outdoors when he feels a tap on his shoulder.

He spins around to find a smiling Neptia Goldstar. The bags they left on Honta are slung over both of her shoulders and she is wearing a weary grin. She starts to open her mouth, most likely with some smart-ass comment on the tip of her tongue, but before she can get a sound out, Tavvi tackles her in a hug.

"You got away!" Tavvi says into her coat.

Neptia lets out a laugh in response.

"Not really! she says. "I just hid until the coast was clear, and then I found you were being held at the station!"

Tavvi pulls away as if to inspect his friend for damage.

She frowns. "I mean I give you credit for trying to 'save' me, but you could have just waited with me in the bushes until the coast was clear!"

"I panicked."

She shakes her head, pulling Tavvi out the train station doors behind her. The stowaways squint against the bright light on Sphe, still unable to believe that they are free.

"Maybe we can just use those smuggling shortcuts to get to another planet instead of waiting for a Goldstar Train," Neptia wonders.

"I want to stay as far as possible from that place," Tavvi replies.

Nep shrugs and saunters off down a predetermined path with Tavvi following after her.

"There isn't much to do here," Neptia notes.

Tavvi chuckles at that. "That hasn't stopped us from finding something to do."

"Yeah! And you're always the one to find 'something!'"

Neptia whacks Tavvi on the arm, and he lets out a guilty laugh.

CHAPTER FOURTEEN

WHEN TAVVI OPENS HIS eyes, he and Neptia are lying next to one another, staring up at a pitch-black sky dotted with stars. Neptia stands up, and Tavvi quickly follows suit.

"Do you ever dream of anything else?" Neptia asks.

"Not sure," Tavvi replies. "All the dreams I can remember having are on this cliff and in your house. And I don't dream every night. I don't think so."

"Everyone dreams," a familiar voice says behind them. "We may not remember it when we wake up, but we do dream."

The duo turns around and finds the woman in white wearing a smile.

"I'm surprised to see you again, Miss Goldstar!" she says, entwining her fingers in front of her. "I thought the previous time I saw you would be the last!"

"Okay, lady," Neptia says, moving in front of Tavvi protectively. "I have had it up to here with the weird dream stuff, this cliff, and..."

She looks around for another thing to get mad about.

"Those stars! We wanna know where Tavvi comes from. NOW! And who the hell are *you*?!"

The smile turns into a frown, and the woman drops her hands to her sides.

"You will find out in due time."

"No, no, NO! No more of the cryptic fortune teller mess!"

Neptia points a finger in her face and scowls.

"I have to agree with her," Tavvi says. "This has gone on long enough."

"That's right!" Neptia exclaims. "We have been running in circles for a solar system and planet that may not even exist! We're trying to find where he comes from. And you are not fucking helping by giving us this...weird, cryptic information! Just give us a straight answer, or stop invading our dreams!"

The woman lets out a deep sigh and turns around, walking a couple of steps closer to the cliff's edge.

"I can't believe you've been traveling with someone this rude," she murmurs in disgust.

"What did you say?!"

The woman turns back toward the duo at the sound of Neptia's indignation.

"The answer is in the tag in his ear. That is the key to finding out who he is and where he comes from."

Tavvi reaches up to cup his hand over his tagged ear.

"But be warned! If you engage or open the tag incorrectly, it will result in an explosion of pure magic that has the force equivalent to an atomic bomb! So, take care!"

Tavvi quickly returns his hand to his side after hearing this information.

"Now, if you'll excuse me."

A brilliant flash of white stings the dreamers' eyes, and the woman is gone, leaving Neptia and Tavvi alone.

"She could have at least woke us up before leaving," Neptia grumbles.

"So...the tag on my ear is...linked to my memories?" Tavvi puzzles out. "How do we know for sure?"

"Only one way to find out! We gotta wake up!" Neptia says determinedly, although Tavvi questions how she can be so sure.

"Wait, so how do we–"

Before he can finish his question, Neptia has him by the shirt and is dragging him to the cliff's edge.

"W-WAIT!" he yelps out. "Nep! What the hell?!"

Neptia pulls him over. They fall, heading straight for the ominous darkness below.

Tavvi sits up in bed, rolling over to warily watch Neptia pop awake like an excited child on Christmas morning. He lets out a terrified and frustrated scream, desperately wiggling away from the ecstatic girl dashing toward him.

"Wait, wait, wait, Nep!!" he yells. "Chill out for a sec!!"

Neptia stops in her tracks, allowing Tavvi a deep groaning sigh.

"Remember what the woman said? If we do this the wrong way, we'll pretty much be detonating a nuke! I don't think we can risk that!"

Neptia shakes her head at him and smiles.

"Don't worry!" she says, reassuringly. "I'm an expert in technology and hacking! How do you think I'm able to do so much on my computer compact? I even hacked into a station terminal once for fun!"

"Are you sure the amount that your family is paying to get you back *isn't* a bounty for your arrest!?"

She ignores the question and climbs into bed beside Tavvi to inspect his tag. She places her left hand on it and runs her thumb along it. Tavvi is a little surprised that the murmurs cannot be heard with Neptia's touch. She turns the tag as much as Tavvi's ear will allow, only to find that it is just two parts stuck with a tight seal, similar to two Legos snapped together.

She tries to pry them apart but cannot quite get her finger in between the two parts. Holding up a finger she leaves the bed to rustle through her bag. Tavvi watches her curiously. However, his curiosity soon changes to fear when she returns to his side with a screwdriver in hand. He lets out a whimper, fully prepared to fight his friend.

"Calm down!" she says, waving her hand flippantly. "I'm going to try and pry it open. Since it's most likely one of those tags we saw in that smuggling room, it *can* be opened. Plus, it looks like I just need the screwdriver anyway, so no big deal."

"W-well...do you have anything else you can–"

"I have an ice pick, a wedge, and–"

"Okay, I'll take the screwdriver! But...what if this goes wrong? What if it detonates and–"

"Tavvi!" Neptia snaps. "Don't you wanna get to the bottom of this? Don't you wanna see where you came from? See your family again and stop running around?"

Tavvi avoids her eyes and lets out a deep sigh.

"Okay, okay, fine," he says. "Just make it quick, okay?"

Neptia nods and leans over him, carefully holding the tag in her left hand and the screwdriver in her right. She wedges the head of the screwdriver into the seal and begins to fidget it left and right, struggling to ignore Tavvi's heavy breathing. She does this motion about six times before the head of the screwdriver breaks the seal.

"Got it!" Neptia cheers.

She looks down at Tavvi to find a stream of tears flowing down his face.

"T-Tavvi?" Neptia whispers. "Are you–"

"Hey, Nep?" Tavvi says calmly. "Could you please finish opening the tag?"

"Did I hurt you? Oh my god, I didn't–"

"I'm fine, Nep. Could you finish opening the tag, please?"

She nods, confident that she can now pry it open with her thumbs. Counting to three, Neptia tugs on both sides of the tag, and after about a minute, it finally pops open.

Unfortunately, the second the tag's seal is released, several green rings encircle Tavvi's body, disembodied voices murmuring and yelling from within. Tavvi freezes in surprise. Neptia dives behind a chair, peeking out at the rings in awe as they slowly begin to shrink around her friend. Meanwhile, Tavvi watches in amazement, his tears now floating above him as the room fills with a magnificent green color. After a moment, a giant flash of green explodes throughout the room, and when Neptia finally rubs the light from her eyes, she finds Tavvi lying on his side on the ground.

She runs from her hiding spot and rushes toward Tavvi, yelling his name. Before she can check his pulse, however, he slowly sits up. His tears begin to flow again, and he speaks with complete confidence:

"Neptia. I finally know who I am and where we have to go."

Chapter Fifteen

Neptia opens her eyes wide and gulps.

"D-do you really know?" she stammers out. "Do you know your real name? Where you came from?"

Tavvi wipes his eyes and smiles.

"My real name is Cayden Quansill," he says confidently. "I'm from the planet Mykeem. In the Harthsil Solar System."

"Cayden...Quansill...Cayden..." She repeats slowly. "I hope you know I'm probably still gonna call you Tavvi 'cuz I've come to know you as that."

Tavvi/Cayden shrugs and stands up. Now with a destination in sight, he begins to pack, finally ready to return home.

Neptia ponders the situation for a second before standing up. Something is not sitting right with her.

"Wait a sec!" Neptia realizes. "The fortune teller told us you were from Rialea in the Nylat Solar System! Someone's lying!"

"I dunno," Tavvi/Cayden shrugs, changing his shirt. "It might have been a bogus reading, but who cares? I'm going home!"

Shaking her head in confusion and anger at the goose chase they had been on, Neptia finally follows suit, packing her belongings and preparing to accompany her friend home. As they finally check out, Neptia heads straight for the station in search of a UPE, Cayden struggling to keep pace. (At this point, the author has decided to refer to Tavvi as Cayden, seeing as that is his actual name and the story is almost finished. Don't worry, however, as Neptia will not be as easily persuaded.)

Upon locating the nearest UPE, Cayden quickly mashes in the coordinates to Mykeem and the planet appears on the screen above as a green and black pixelated drawing.

"That's it?" Neptia asks.

Cayden nods and manages to pay the fee with a few stray bills from his backpack. After a few moments, the doors open and the duo steps in. The device resembles a normal elevator with its red carpet and bright white light above. However, the Universal Planet Elevator rattles a bit, reciting fun facts and destination times. As the rattling slows to a dull clatter, the doors finally slide open with a chirpy: "Welcome to Mykeem!"

Report on Mykeem...incoming...hold on...ready...

Mykeem is the fourth planet in the Harthstil Solar System. However, despite being one of the more populous solar systems in the galaxy, it can only be reached by UPEs found at your local stations.

Mykeem is another one of the many planets in the galaxy that contain earth-like properties and fit the Goldilock Zone's criteria for life. Come to think of it...most, if not all, of the planets in the Harthstil Solar System are earth-like and can sustain life! It's a perfect place to live! Strange...

Anyway...

Not much is known about Mykeem other than the rumor that Mykeem was terraformed from a desolate desert planet by Mages in a single day. The source of these claims is sadly unknown.

For more information about Mykeem, please visit our site, as some information may not be available on the planet...

Neptia and Cayden exit the elevator to find themselves outside of a local terrestrial train station.

"I'm finally home," Cayden says with a smile. "It's been too long."

"Not a bad planet," Neptia notes, stretching. "Seems comfy."

Cayden hails a taxi and gives the driver the address of his house as they climb in. He soon sinks into the seat and sighs.

"My house isn't that far," he informs Neptia. "But walking there would take a few hours."

Nepita nods and stares out the window at the planet's population walking the streets. Endless buildings flip by as she blinks.

"What are you going to do when you get back home?" Neptia asks, turning back toward Cayden.

"I'm probably gonna go back to my normal life," he says. "I was in college after all. What about you?"

"I guess I'll go back to riding the Goldstar Line."

Cayden snaps around and looks at Neptia, concerned.

"You're really going to leave after all we've been through?" he asks.

Neptia only nods, unable to meet Cayden's eyes.

"You found where you belong," she explains. "That was the end goal. There's no point in me staying behind since you're back home. My home is on the Goldstar Line,"

"But you can come live with me! You could even go to school."

"I don't wanna go to school. It sucks. I don't even know what I'd want to major in."

"I could help you."

"No thanks."

"Nep, I'm literally giving you a free house to live in and you're gonna say no?! Nep, please!"

"I said no, Tavvi! I'm one of the most wanted people in the galaxy right now! You don't need all that in your house! I know I wouldn't..."

Tavvi lets out a sigh and rubs his face.

"I guess you have a point there."

As their conversation concludes, the taxi slows down, stopping in front of Cayden's home They find themselves in front of a pure white marble mansion. A green hedge surrounds the property, with a burbling fountain sitting amongst the greenery between the mansion and the road. Neptia opens her eyes, her jaw slack as she points at the mansion.

"Y-you're rich?!" she stammers out. She doesn't mean to be rude, but Cayden does not exactly act as though he was raised with high society etiquette.

Cayden lets out a laugh, walking forward with no hesitation.

"Kind of," he says. "We inherited it from my grandparents, and my mom's been working hard to make sure we keep it."

They enter the hedge and walk through a garden filled with strange and foreign plant life. Upon reaching the door, Cayden hesitates before knocking and backing away to stand in silence. After a moment, the door slowly creeks open to reveal a somewhat young-looking woman wearing a gold and red dress. Her sky-black hair is tied in a bun and adorned with golden accessories.

Cayden holds his arms out with a bright smile.

"Hi, Mom!"

The words have barely left his mouth before his mother rushes into his arms and hugs him, almost knocking him over as she cries into his shoulder.

"C-Cayden!" she sobs. "Oh, I missed you so, so, so much! Where have you been? I know you like to wander, but I've been so worried."

"I missed you too, Mom! But I'm safe now!"

She looks up from his shoulder to catch sight of Neptia. Neptia awkwardly waves hello, but Cayden's mother has already released her son in order to scoop his friend into a hug.

"Thank you!" she murmurs. "Thank you so much for keeping my Cayden safe!"

She lets go of Neptia and shakes her head in disapproval at herself.

"Oh, my goodness. Here we are out in the open crying and hugging like no one else is on the planet! Come in, you two!"

The duo follows her inside of the mansion where they are met with a beautiful gold and red medley of statues and vases. Each spacious room is perfectly adorned with a variety of these decorations.

"Go and get washed up. Then you both can come down for something to eat. You still like ham, right Caycay?"

"Caycay?" Neptia snickers.

Cayden quickly shuts her up with a whack to the arm.

"Yeah, ham sounds nice, Mom!"

Cayden's mother claps her hands and a maid appears to show Neptia to her room where she can clean up. Cayden leaves his suitcase by the door and dashes into his own room. After a long and deserving shower, he stands in awe of his bedroom, still filled with trophies, posters, and photos just the way he left them. He crosses the room to his dresser to pick up a framed photo of him and his mother at his high school graduation. He laughs out loud, remembering his mom crying like a baby despite the fact that he still had a few more months to go until he left for college.

"Tavvi!"

Cayden almost drops the photo as he jumps around to find Neptia standing in a robe, her hair pulled back.

"What's up? I wanted to see how–. Oh, you still have that tag in your ear," she interrupts herself, pointing at the splintered pieces dangling from where she popped it open earlier. "When are you going to take that out?"

He sets the photo down and fumbles to pull at the tag, huffing as it sticks and Neptia laughs out loud at his frustration.

"Don't worry about it!" she says, waving an arm. "It'll probably fall out eventually."

He sighs, looking at Neptia.

"So...when are you going to leave?" he asks.

She looks around at the awards and memories lining Cayden's walls, deep in thought.

"Probably in the middle of the night when everyone's sleeping," she decides.

"The middle of the night?! You're not even gonna wait until the morning to say goodbye?!"

She shakes her head at that question. Cayden opens his mouth to speak, but she holds a finger in front of his face.

"Tavvi," she says firmly, slowly dropping her hand and sighing. "Remember? I'm one of the most wanted people in the galaxy! I need to keep a low profile so I won't get arrested, or worse, taken back to my family! So, it's best for me to slip out unnoticed. I'm sorry."

Cayden looks down at the floor, a look of deep concern and sadness on his face. His expression is quickly broken by a few condescending/reassuring pats on the head from Neptia.

"You can say goodbye before I leave if you want. I'll probably let you know before I go to bed."

Cayden opens his mouth to object again, but he is cut off by someone knocking on the door. With permission, a butler enters. He informs them that dinner is ready, and they may come down whenever they wish. Neptia follows him out of the room, evidently eager for a change of clothes and a hot meal.

After he finally musters the courage to face his mother, Cayden leaves his room only to run into Neptia in the hall. They walk to the dining room together and find Cayden's mother sitting at the head of a decently sized table.

"Oh!" Cayden's mother exclaims as they sit down on either side of her. "I should have said earlier. My name is Gianna. I was so happy to see my little Cay that I completely forgot to introduce myself!"

"I know your name, Mom," Cayden says jokingly.

"I should hope so!"

Gianna claps her hands and servers flood the room, bringing food and drink for the three of them. The food set in front of them includes the meat of an Amara Boar, a type of wild pig only found in the Harthsil Solar System that when cooked properly for five to six hours, removes any sort of gaminess that turns many away from the pig. Alongside the meat lay Ginrum berries. Freshly picked and grilled green with a hint of blue they produce a savory green flavor when cooked immediately after being picked or develop a tart sweetness the longer they ripen. Beside this lavish food is a simple side of mashed potatoes with red tomato gravy.

Cayden and Neptia do not waste any time digging into their meal, but Gianna only looks on with a joyful smile as she sips a deep red wine.

"I can't thank you enough for bringing my Cayden back home," Gianna says to Neptia. "Would you like to stay here with us? I can give you a very good job or even an education if you'd like!"

"No thank you," Neptia politely declines. "I need to get back to my own job and family."

Cayden interrupts his next mouthful of dinner to shoot his friend a critical look.

"Really?" Gianna is interested now. "And where do you work?"

"Well, I work at a souvenir shop on Lethum. That's how I found him." She gestures to Cayden.

"Was your boss okay with you just getting up and leaving your job to go travel around space with a random stranger?"

Cayden looks over at Neptia, slightly concerned, but Neptia only takes a drink of water and clears her throat.

"Oh, I run the store alone," she says calmly. "And the store's not open year-round. So, me closing it up for a few weeks or a month isn't out of the ordinary."

"You run a shop by yourself? Color me impressed!"

Cayden lets out a sigh of relief, still in disbelief that his mother fell for that lie.

"Cayden!" Gianna says, snapping his attention to her. "After all this time you've been gone, I need to ask: can you still perform your magic?"

"Of course, Mom!"

He holds his middle and index finger close together and a white flame appears from between them like a reflex. Gianna imitates his movements, copying him perfectly. Neptia looks on in awe.

"That's good and all, but I mean the serious stuff," Gianna says, standing up. "C'mon! Let's show your friend what we can do!"

"Oh Mom, I don't know if Nep would be okay with—"

"You don't mind, do you, dear?"

Neptia smiles brightly, intrigued by the situation playing out before her.

"I don't mind!" she says.

Cayden looks slightly concerned but quickly shakes his head, smiles, and runs to Gianna's side.

"So, what type of magic is this?" Neptia questions. "Like coin tricks or–"

Before she can finish, a burst of flame erupts from Cayden and Gianna's hands, drawing a loud gasp from their guest's lips. The fire soon turns to a stream of ice. Cayden quickly breaks away to crouch on the ground as Gianna backs away. A glacier shoots out of the floor below him and he is flung into the air. As he falls back to the ground, the glacier turns into a small tree. Cayden hits the top of the tree feet-first, his touch causing it to turn into a storm of multicolored flower petals that flutter around the dining room, eventually vanishing to leave the three of them alone.

Neptia stands and claps while Gianna looks on and nods, amused. Cayden bows and returns to his plate as though he did not just perform a whole show.

"Are you guys in the circus or something?!" Neptia asks, still in awe.

"Well, not really, dear," Gianna says, almost laughing as she rejoins her son and guest at the table. "You see, the planets in this solar system: Nomathra, Mykeem, Yolaga, Themsal, Dramalga, and Aqualac, in that order of course, were found to have gems near the core of the planet. I believe they are called aquila crystals, and they radiate some sort of strange energy that we have yet to identify. Now, when you are exposed to this energy from the crystals for long periods of time, - about five-or-so years - you will slowly gain the powers that you saw me and Cayden use."

She lets out a chuckle and takes a sip of water.

"Perhaps if you would like to live with us for a bit, maybe we could teach you some magic and–"

Her attention has now shifted to Cayden who seems oblivious to everything but the meal in front of him.

"Cayden, what's that in your ear?"

The mood quickly turns sour as Neptia's bemused face morphs into concern. Cayden lets out a sigh.

"Mom, I don't want you to worry, but...I think the reason I was gone for so long was...well, I think I was trafficked."

"WHAT?!" Gianna stands and confronts Cayden directly. "How in the galaxy did you come up with that idea?!"

Cayden begins his tale of following the woman with a similar tag to a hidden room filled with suitcases. The story continues on for a while, ending with Cayden's reacquisition of his memories by opening the tag. Gianna does not speak a word throughout the entire story, and as it ends, she simply walks over to Cayden and hugs him.

Finally pulling away, she inspects the device still dangling from his ear and murmurs, "release," catching it as it falls into her hand. She then places a bittersweet kiss on her son's forehead.

"I am so sorry, Cayden," she says, making her way out of the dining room and to the front door of her home.

Gianna only pauses in the doorway once to explain. "I need to call the authorities to report this. I won't be back for the rest of the evening. Please don't interrupt dinner on my behalf. However, when the meal is through, I want you two to stay in your rooms until the police arrive. They might need to question you both."

Cayden and Neptia sit alone in silence for a moment before Nepta grabs her glass of water and breaks the silence.

"That was weird."

"Yeah," Cayden agrees.

He rubs the lobe of his ear where the tag was attached for so long.

"I'm a bit freaked out by how she just acted," Neptia says. "That was so out of the blue."

"I guess? But, maybe she was so scared about what I've been through that she couldn't wait until morning to contact the authorities."

"Okay, but how the hell did she know how to pop off the tag?"

"Maybe she's run into this before, I mean, she knows how to do all kinds of things."

Neptia thinks about this for a second and shrugs.

"That could be a possibility, but just be careful, okay? That was just an odd choice of actions."

Cayden nods in an attempt to placate his friend. After dinner, the duo return to their respective rooms. Before they part ways, however, Cayden lets out a sigh and glances at Neptia.

"I guess this is it, huh?" he says.

Neptia nods and closes the space between them to give Cayden a hug. He hugs her back as tight as he can.

"Goodbye, Neptia," Cayden whispers, fighting back tears.

"Bye, Tavvi," she replies, also struggling to hold back her emotions. "Good luck in your life, no matter where you go. And if you can, try and ride the Goldstar Line, okay? I'll be there."

Chapter Sixteen

The shuffling of feet pulls Neptia from her sleep. It is not loud enough to pry her eyes open until she hears it again. She rolls onto her back, popping an eye open to stare blankly at the ceiling. She glances down without moving her head and sees a shadow standing at the foot of her bed.

"Tavvi?" she says quietly.

The shadow does not say anything. She props up her upper body on her elbows and reaches for the lamp.

"Tavvi, I told you a million times. I'm not–"

Click.

The lamp illuminates the room, and Neptia is now wide awake. The creature in the room is not her friend. It is only a shadow with no discernable features. Neptia lets out a loud screech and grabs a book on the bedside table, throwing it at the being. The creature dodges the projectile by phasing through it, moving so fast it appears as though there are two of them.

Seeming irritated, it dashes toward Neptia, moving on all fours. Neptia gasps and helplessly chucks the nearest item on her night table. The creature manages to catch the makeshift weapon, but before it can return the favor, sparks of electricity arc out from the object. Soon, the shadow is shocked by what seems to be a million volts of electricity, finally collapsing on the ground after several minutes.

Neptia dashes out of bed, grabbing the item she threw - the top half of her computer compact that she modified to act like a taser - from the floor. Not wasting a moment, she snatches the bottom half of the device from the bedside table and runs for Cayden's door, desperately yelling for him. When Cayden opens his door, he is greeted by a panicked Neptia diving into his arms.

"T-TAVVI!" Neptia screams out, pointing at her room. "T-There was someone in my room! I managed to take them down but-"

She is gasping for breath, but Cayden only blinks at her, confused.

"Nep," he grumbles. "Are you sure you weren't just having a bad dream?"

"No, I wasn't! There was a very real-"

She looks behind Cayden's shoulder into his room and sees another shadow exactly like the one in her room. She screams and points behind him. Cayden whirls around just in time to shoot a fireball at the shadow as it sprints at the two of them with an unnatural gait. Luckily, as the fireball makes impact, the shadow creature collapses instantly.

"I told you!" Neptia says. "We need to get the hell out of here!"

They sprint for the front door of the manor in only their pajamas, but the faster they run, the farther the door appears to be. Neptia wonders if she is dreaming; it is like running on a treadmill going backward, and they are never fast enough to escape. Shaking the thought from her head, Neptia takes a running leap at the doors, but as she is midair, an invisible force slams both her and Cayden into the back wall. The force prevents them from breaking free, even as they struggle.

"You can't leave yet," a voice chimes from all around.

A gust of wind blows through the corridors, forming a red and white tornado of ribbons in front of the hostages. Then, in a brilliant flash, Gianna materializes in front of them with several masked individuals behind her.

"I'm terribly sorry, but you two can't leave just yet," Gianna repeats calmly.

"Why the fuck not?!" Neptia yells.

"Because I haven't got the ransom ready yet, dear!"

"Ransom?" Cayden asks. "What the hell are you talking about, Mom?"

"Oh, my dear Cayden," Gianna says, smiling. "I knew that story about your friend running a shop was a load of nonsense. I know that she's Neptia Goldstar and there's a massive reward for bringing her back home safely!"

She walks over and cups Cayden's face in her hands.

"Now imagine that price doubled when they find out that she's been kidnapped by an individual who's *also* wanted in most of the galaxy!"

Cayden's eyes open wide as his mother drops her hands from his face.

"Mom!" he cries out. "Are you going to frame me as–"

"As Neptia's kidnapper? Yes! I'll make it look like you kidnapped Goldstar over here, and when the Goldstar family turns up to collect her, you'll get arrested, and I'll make the money for turning you in!"

"It won't work!" Neptia argues. "Tavvi would never–"

"Oh, I'm aware of that," Gianna says, grabbing the top of Neptia's nightgown. "That's why they won't be getting the real one. It won't be that hard to make a duplicate of you."

A portal opens at Gianna's side, and Neptia is carefully plucked from the wall by the unseen force.

"After all, it's the *least* you could do for messing up a couple of my trading stations!"

Cayden's eyes grow wide as the connection is made.

"Y-You're in the trafficking business?!" He yells, his voice echoing around them. "What the fuck is wrong with you?!" How can you do something- Wait...Are you the one who put me into the smudging ring?!"

"You ask too many questions."

With a flick of her arm, she throws Neptia into the portal.

"NEPTIA!"

Cayden uses all his power to break free of the wall and make a dive for the portal. Gianna's masked army rushes to grab him, but they are too late.

Report on EGL-8467 incoming...hold on...wait a moment. ..almost ready...incoming...

EGL-8467 is a planet in an unknown solar system that is very near to a dying sun. While the planet itself is not deadly, the air surrounding it is extremely poisonous. If a healthy being remains on this planet for upwards of three to four hours, it can send them into a coma, and if not treated, death is almost certain. The IRTD requires more information about this planet and its solar system.

If you or someone you know has information about this planet, please contact the IRTD immediately, as any information is crucial to the research and possible terraforming of this planet.

Cayden tumbles through the portal and lands on the planet facedown. He groans and looks up to find Neptia in the same position as the portal closes above them. Her body is lifeless.

"NEPTIA!" Cayden cries out and rushes to her.

He gently lifts her upper body into his arms and places a bubble of breathable air around her head. After a moment, her body gasps for air, and she opens her eyes to find Cayden on the verge of tears.

"Tavvi?" she mumbles.

He nods, tears filling his eyes.

"O-oh god, Nep," he sobs. "I am so, so, sorry for getting us into this! This was all my fault! We shouldn't have tried to make it back to my home. We should have just kept traveling on the Goldstar Line! I'm so sorry for getting you chased by the police and..."

She covers his mouth with her hand and smiles before slowly standing up.

"It's fine," she says reassuringly. "You lost your memories. You didn't know that your mom was in that type of business."

Cayden rises to his feet and the two of them look out across the desolate planet.

"Now what?" Cayden says. "We need to get back to the mansion before your family gets scammed and I get framed!"

"Can't you just open up a portal like her?" Neptia asks.

In response, Cayden crouches on the balls of his feet, looking into the distance.

"I can't," he admits. "My powers aren't that strong. Hell, I don't even know a spell to create a portal."

Then, like an answer to their dilemma, another portal opens a few feet away. Cayden stands up and summons a fireball in preparation for one of Gianna's minions. A leg dangles out of the portal and–

It's Rayard wearing a protective suit.

He looks to his left and is taken aback at the sight of *those two* here. He rubs his eyes and– yep, that's Neptia Goldstar and the stowaway who miraculously escaped his clutches during their last encounter.

"The fuck!?" Ray says aloud. "What the-how the...what the hell are you two doing here?!"

Neptia steps forward to confront Ray, but Cayden inserts himself between the officer and his friend to explain the situation. Surprisingly, Ray listens and nods thoughtfully before turning to his still-open portal. After hearing the story, the windfall for Neptia's return seems to be the last thing on his mind.

"You two need to come with me. Now!"

They are a bit reluctant, but remaining on the planet would be a death sentence. They follow Ray into the portal and tumble out the other side into the empty local station on Mykeem.

"How did you know we'd be there?" Neptia asks.

"I didn't," Ray says, helping Cayden up as his protective suit collapses into his back, forming a square backpack. "I know that Hearthsil trafficking victims often end up there, and I like to check on that planet when I have a free moment. I don't want anyone dying out there on my watch."

Neptia shoots to her feet and heads for the exit as soon as Ray extends a hand to her.

"We need to stop Gianna before she tricks my family and Tavvi's framed for my kidnapping!"

Just as she begins to pick up the pace, Cayden grabs Neptia's shoulder and pulls her back in front of him.

"You need to stay here, Nep," he says. "I'll deal with my mom."

"No!" Neptia protests. "We went into this as a team, and we'll finish this as a team! Let me come with you!"

"Do you know any magic, Nep?!"

Neptia stares at him blankly before looking down and shaking her head.

"My mom is a powerful mage, and if we both attack her, she'll most likely kill you! I understand you want to help me, but I need to do this alone. I'm sorry Nep, but you need to stay here."

She hugs him, and as he pulls away, she nods toward the exit.

"Wait," Ray says.

Cayden stops and turns to look at his friend and the officer.

"Before you go, I need to tell you something. Ray swallows hard and takes a deep breath. I'm the one that woke you up from your suitcase."

"What?!" Cayden did not think this night could be any more surprising. "How?!"

"There were reports of a suspicious suitcase on a bench left in a station. Since I was the closest officer, I responded and went to investigate. When I opened it, there you were, huddled in the fetal position. It looked like you had been scuffed up in a fight, but you were still breathing, so I called for medical back at my booth.

"When I turned back around, you were gone. I didn't see you again, with the exception of a couple of calls from other stations and some grainy footage. Then the wanted posters of you and Neptia started popping up, and my partner Verla and I started chasing after you."

Cayden can only blink in shock. This was the guy who had woken him up and saved him from a horrible life. Maybe he misjudged the officer that had been hunting him for weeks.

"I'm really sorry for chasing after you two. Blame orders and me wanting money and fame and whatnot.

He quickly changes his tone. "Now go! Hurry!" Go before I actually have to arrest you!"

Cayden nods and charges out of the station, leaving Ray and Neptia alone.

Chapter Seventeen

Cayden snakes his way through the dark streets of My-keem, following the familiar path to the home he grew up in. Dawn breaks as rage and betrayal flow through his body. How could his own mother be a part of this?

It finally hits him as he reaches the neighborhood and sees the mansion from down the street. The smuggling ring was probably the only way his mother could afford to keep that fancy piece of land in her ownership. Even if there was an inheritance involved, there was no way her job as a translator could continuously afford this type of home and lifestyle.

As he reaches his childhood home, Cayden slips through the hedge, dashes across the front garden, and throws the front door open. Waiting for him on the other side is a being wearing a mask. A second hooded figure attempts to intercept him as the masked being shoots a fireball.

Cayden is taken aback by the sudden attack, but he instinctively grabs the fireball with his right hand and absorbs it. He then turns it into a burst of flame and shoots it back at the two beings, causing them to catch on fire and vanish.

Familiars, Cayden says to himself, recalling the name from one of his mother's lessons.

He shakes his head and dashes upstairs to his mother's office where he beats down the flimsily locked door. The room is completely dark except for the early morning light beaming through a single window. Gianna's silhouette stands in front of a stately table, a communication device pressed to her ear. Her back is turned, and Cayden can barely make out her demand for more reinforcements before she ends the conversation and turns around, resting her hands behind her on the table.

"Color me impressed, Cayden!" Gianna says cheerfully. "I thought you wouldn't make it off that planet alive!"

Cayden throws a fireball at her in response. She vanishes before it can make contact, reappearing in front of her son with her hand around his throat. Throwing her weight forward, she slams him to the ground with so much force, he is pretty sure it makes a dent.

"I'll have you know, I can just kill you by doing this over and over again, my dear," Gianna states, her hand still clenched around his throat. "And, being quite frank, I'm okay with that,"

Cayden lets out a yell and grabs her throat in retaliation. He propels her to the back of the room, slamming her into the wall. He attempts to pin her there, but she quickly shoves him away and lobs several fireballs at his head. He summons a pulsing blue shield to protect him only to realize too late that the fireballs were a distraction.

Before he can blink, she is dashing toward him, cackling like a madman. He panics, losing all control for a moment as his hands shoot out a bolt of electricity. By some fortune, it hits her, sending her sprawling to the ground.

She wastes no time in leaping to her feet, laughing as she eyes the ice blade her son has just summoned.

"You haven't lost your touch, even if you forgot you could even use magic for a few months!" Gianna says between giggles. "I wonder what sort of damage you could have done during a war somewhere!"

"What the fuck are you talking about?!" Cayden exclaims, holding out his frozen blade.

Gianna stops laughing and wipes her eyes.

"I'm pretty sure you made the connection, but you were smuggled, dear. You were supposed to be fighting a war somewhere. Sold to be someone's bodyguard! That's the whole reason we do this! Imagine the power you've just shown!

"Do you have any idea how much people will pay for that?! Imagine that magic in a war somewhere! Whoever has that will most certainly win and will be able to acquire anything for it!"

Cayden clenches his free hand and tears form in his eyes.

"Why?" he asks, quietly.

"Excuse me?"

Cayden throws the blade at her, but she swiftly dodges it.

"Why me?! Why the fuck was I chosen to be part of this dumb little ring of yours?!"

"BECAUSE WE WERE SHORT!"

She vanishes and appears in front of him, gripping his shoulders.

"Let me explain this to you," she says, looking at him directly. "We just needed some extra tags to ship out and I was more than willing to sacrifice you to help."

She walks around Cayden's back, tracing a finger along his shoulder as he stands frozen.

"Plus, I got a couple extra bucks just for the trouble of sending you off, dear."

Cayden bites his lower lip and lets out an extremely loud scream. It's so loud, in fact, that it creates a shockwave that breaks all of the windows in the house and sends Gianna flying out of the room and down the stairs to the first floor below.

She hits the ground with a thud, desperately trying to regain her footing. She finally looks up, catching sight of Cayden crouching on the railing above her, his eyes full of tears. He summons another blade of ice and lunges off the railing.

She glares up at him and vanishes, leaving her son to land where she lay only seconds before. Cayden turns around and slashes at his mother as she reappears, but she steps back, blocking the blade with her left arm.

"This has gone on for long enough!" Gianna yells.

A brilliant white flash from many of Cayden's dreams throws him back to the ground. When he opens his eyes against the stinging light, Gianna has transformed into a perfect replica of the woman in his dreams. She begins to sing an opera song and ice particles appear around her. The particles become icicles that fly at Cayden as the woman in white lets out a howling screech.

He rolls out of the way and quickly regains his footing to dodge her attack. In an attempt to protect himself, Cayden summons a cluster of fireballs around him and shoots them out at his attacker. Gianna manages to absorb and dodge all but one.

Her footing is off and a fireball catches her in the stomach, sending her to the floor screaming in pain before finally falling quiet. Her brilliant white form stutters, returning to normal. Cayden's choice of weaponry is a fire blade this time. He summons it as he approaches her, unsure if that was all it took to take her down.

He leans over Gianna, unable to see the rise and fall of her chest. Near tears, Cayden reaches out to his mother.

Gianna sits up and grabs Cayden by the throat, glaring at him. She slowly stands up, raising him into the air with her grip.

"I'm not sure who or what woke you up," she growls, aggravated. "But I'll find and kill them myself. Slowly."

She turns back into the white woman and throws Cayden into the wall. Fires an ice cycle at him, she holds his body in place with an unseen force. He almost dodges, but his arm is too slow. The weapon nicks his bicep, causing a stream of blood to run down his arm and drip off his fingertips. Gianna walks up to him slowly, summoning a dozen more icicles that circle behind her.

"I wonder if you can dodge a few more," she says thoughtfully.

Cayden stares into her eyes and realizes that this is it for him. He closes his own eyes, grateful that he did find out who he was. Throughout his journey, he uncovered a major trading and smuggling ring, so he didn't feel it was *all* in vain.

He met someone who showed him a part of the galaxy he would have never seen. They ate some wonderful foods and saw things he had never imagined. Cayden made a deeper connection with his friend than he ever thought possible.

He takes a deep breath, and with a smile on his face and tears flowing from his eyes, waits for the icicles to pierce him.

BeepBeepBeepBEEEEEP!

What was that?

Cayden opens his eyes at the new sound.

"What the hell?" Gianna exclaims, returning to her terrestrial form and looking around in confusion.

BeepBeepBeepBEEEEEEP!

Mother and son turn their heads upward to find several black and white sphere-shaped drones surrounding both of them.

"Oh, for fucks sake!" Gianna yells out, annoyed.

She flies off to somewhere in the mansion with the drones right behind her. Not even a minute later, a couple of armed soldiers enter the mansion and head straight to Cayden gently pulling him down from where he is still being held to the wall.

"Do you need medical care?" one of them asks.

Cayden shakes his head and dusts himself off.

"Follow us."

Cayden does as he is told. He wonders if this is part of his magic or a near-death vision but quickly dismisses the thought. As they exit the mansion and converge in the garden, he is met with a smiling Neptia. She appears to have been crying amongst the soldiers and various hovercrafts clearing the area.

"N-Nep?!" Cayden yells out. "I-is that–"

"Yep. It's me, Tavvi," she replies.

"How did you– Did you even– How–"

She approaches him and reaches into his pocket, pulling out her computer compact. She opens it to show Cayden the current screen it is frozen on.

"I snuck it into your pocket when you hugged me," Neptia explains. "It's been recording ever since, and with Ray's help, I managed to get it connected to a radio and a communicator and we listened to you and your mom. Then Ray called Special Forces and–"

Neptia's explanation is cut off by Cayden's hug. She returns the hug, wrapping her arms around him and burying her face in his shoulder. They break apart as a black and gold hovering limo lands on the street.

"That looks familiar," Neptia says.

Two people hop out of the limo and open a door on either side of the vehicle. A man wearing a suit and a woman wearing a black pantsuit climb out, and Neptia covers her mouth at the sight of them.

"Mom?!" she calls. "Dad?!"

Her mother locks her eyes on her daughter and runs to scoop her into her arms. Neptia's father is not far behind.

"Oh, Neptia! We found you," her mother cries. "Are you okay?! We got the news from the station and came to find you."

"I'm fine, Mom," Neptia says, waving her off. She gestures to her friend. "This is Tavvi."

"Nice to meet you," her father says politely, extending his hand

Neptia's mother seems almost hysterical as she begins to apologize and bargain with her daughter.

"Neptia, I am so sorry for trying to force you into the family business and not listening to what you wanted!"

"And, um," her father chimes in. "I'm sorry for not listening as well. I should have stood up for you."

"Can you ever forgive us?" her mother questions.

Neptia glances around at the expectant faces.

"No," she says calmly.

"Neptia, why?!" her mother wails.

"You guys never listened to what I wanted to do, and you only forced me into things that *you* wanted me to. You never asked if I was okay, and I was really stressed, and that's why I kept getting expelled! I felt like I had no other choice than to run away."

She looks down as her mother places a hand on her shoulder.

"Oh, Neptia..."

"I'm not coming back home."

Her mother sighs but gently lifts Neptia's chin up with her finger.

"Well...you're an adult now...You can do whatever you want–"

The reunion is interrupted by a yelp as several droids drag Gianna out of the front door. The once spherical flying machines have become a sort of funky fashion statement with several decorating her neck and holding her arms together. They gently tug her toward Verla, who has arrived as backup.

Gianna catches sight of Cayden and Neptia and struggles against her bonds.

"CAYDEN!" she yells out, enraged. "This isn't over! I'll be getting out very soon, and You'll regret it when I do!"

"Yeah, it's over," Verla says, crossing her arms. "Those things are not coming off, no matter how much you yell for vengeance."

Gianna is hauled into a police ship that quickly departs for another planet.

Neptia's father clears his throat to recapture the attention of his daughter and her friend.

"Anyway," he speaks up. "We'll work on getting both of you pardoned so that you can travel around without the authorities stopping you every time you land on a planet."

"Thank you, sir," Cayden says.

Reluctant to leave, Neptia's parents shower her with affection and thank Cayden for keeping her safe. As they finally reboard their limo and fly away, Neptia can only wave goodbye. Cayden turns around to find an officer approaching them, backpacks in their hands.

"Okay, you two are free to go," he says, handing them their bags "And if we need you guys for any more information about this case, we'll call you."

Neptia and Tavvi nod in understanding as they are escorted out of the mansion's front garden. Neptia stretches her arms and looks to Cayden.

"Now what?" she asks.

"Weren't you going to leave me?" Cayden asks. "You *did* say that."

She shrugs at the question.

"I think I'm just gonna stay with you. Without you, I'd be dead or in a worse situation. It's the least I can do."

Tavvi chuckles as Neptia smiles.

"I'm hungry," she finally says. "Do you know anywhere we could eat?"

"There's this place nearby I always go to after school. They make really good curry noodles."

"Sounds good! Oh shoot, we're still in our pj's."

Cayden looks down at what he's wearing as Neptia lets out a giggle.

"We should probably find a place to change before we go and–"

"Nep, I almost got killed by my mother," Cayden interjects. "I think the people at the restaurant can stand to watch a person in their pajamas eat for a little bit."

"Fine."

EPILOGUE

IT'S BEEN A LITTLE over six months since Neptia and Cayden returned to his home planet. They still ride the Goldstar Train together and visit various planets when Cayden has a moment to get away from his college classes. The only difference now is that they have an actual home on Honta they can retire to when the traveling becomes too much.

As for Ray and Verla, they are still working as station officers. The two duos have become close friends. They always chat for a bit when they happen to run into each other between stations. As for Gianna (if anyone is even worried about her), she is currently sitting in a maximum-security prison somewhere, pending her trial. Some of the charges she has racked up include human trafficking, attempted murder, and kidnapping.

Cayden is dreaming yet again. He wakes up in that cave on the cliff that started so many problems. He sits up and walks out to the edge to look up, where he is met with only stars glimmering in the distance. There is no moon like in his previous dreams.

"This dream again?" Neptia asks, walking up next to him.

Cayden nods, not breaking his attention from the sky.

"Hey, what's that?" Neptia wonders, pointing to something beyond the cliff.

Cayden follows Neptia's finger and sees the glittering of distant lights, like houses in a little village.

"That's never been there before," Cayden notes.

They watch as a bridge forms. One end connects to the cliff and leads into the distance.

"Let's go check it out!" Neptia decides, smiling. "C'mon!"

She runs across the bridge as Cayden looks on and smiles. He never thought that his life would take him here: finding out his mother was the head of an illegal smuggling ring, being chased by two cops, one of which saved him from being shipped out to war somewhere in the galaxy, and traveling the universe with the former heiress to the very train they ride on to this day.

And after all that, he finally realizes that he will never have to worry about being alone. He'll always have Neptia by his side, and that is good enough for him.

"Tavvi!"

He snaps out of his trance to find Neptia standing in the middle of the bridge.

"Are you coming or what?!" she yells back.

"I'm on my way, Nep!"

About the Author

Trisha "Ninja" Shaw is a writer that currently lives somewhere close to Annapolis. When she's not checking out customers at her bookstore job or telling them why they should read Erin Morgenstern, she can be found writing about whatever comes to her mind. "Neptia's Galaxy Railway" Is her first published book. You can follow her Bluesky, Instagram, Tiktok, and Medium @Ninjaswriting for book updates, samples of upcoming projects, and her little rambles.